MW00744037

Lilacs
&
Bifocals
Shirley Bigelow DeKelver

LILACS & BIFOCALS

by

Shirley Bigelow DeKelver

Cover Art:
MLC Designs 4U

Publisher's Note:

This is a work of fiction. All names, characters, places, and events are the work of the author's imagination.

Any resemblance to real persons, places, or events is coincidental.

Solstice Publishing - www.solsticepublishing.com

Dedicated to the memories of my parents, Sidney and Dimphena Bigelow.

Prologue

Caroline woke with a start. A cold draft swept across her bed and an overwhelming aroma of lilacs filled her room.

A sudden movement caught the corner of her eye, where a dark shadow floated across the room and stopped at the foot of her bed. She watched in disbelief as it manifested into the form of a beautiful woman dressed in a white flowing gown. Her dark eyes stared deeply into Caroline's. Around the woman's neck was a glowing locket, pulsating as if it had a heart of its own.

"The truth is buried in the past," the spectre whispered, "but the answer lies in the future." Then the ghostly body shifted and slowly rose wraithlike towards the ceiling and disappeared.

Caroline closed her eyes tightly, but the scent of lilacs lingered, and she knew with a certainty what she had just witnessed was not a dream.

She lay awake for hours, shivering uncontrollably under the covers, unable to get the vision and the message out of her head. Something troubled her and just as she started to drift off to sleep, she sat up quickly, her heart pounding. The locket around the spirit's neck was identical to the one Grandma had given her when she was a small girl.

What was the message the ethereal visitor was trying to deliver? Was it a warning of some kind? Was something dreadful going to happen?

Chapter 1
Stray Heifer and Mysterious Meadow

It was an unseasonably warm fall, and a few shrunken berries hung wearily on the branches of a Saskatoon bush, soon to be picked clean by migrating birds.

Caroline Lindstrom encouraged Ebony, her black quarter horse, to pick up his pace. The twigs and shrubbery brushed against his withers while the dried leaves disturbed by his passing drifted gently to the ground.

Turning down one of the steep side trails, they eventually arrived at Hunter's Creek. Water trickled sluggishly over the slick rocks, creating a small waterfall as it spilled into a natural pool. The decomposed trunk of a white birch which had toppled years ago was lying half-submerged in the stream.

Caroline dismounted, stretching her tired muscles. She took a drink of water from her canteen and hung it back on the saddle horn.

Eagle Mountain was used by the ranchers for free-range grazing. In the fall, the cattle were rounded up to collect late calves and to separate the spring calves from their mothers for weaning. After the steers were driven to the holding corrals located in a clearing half-way down the mountain, they were separated by brand and then counted.

They were missing a heifer and Grandpa had sent Caroline back up the trail to see if she could find the stray in the heavy bush. If it was not found soon, the search would have to be called off as they had to get the rest of the herd down the mountain before nightfall. As she rode away, Caroline overheard Grandpa telling Pete, their hired hand, that it was going to be a hard winter, and they could not afford to lose even one cow.

She had been riding since dawn and was exhausted

and thirsty. Normally, she looked forward to spending hours riding Ebony, but lately she had been waking up in the middle of the night, tossing and turning for hours before falling back to sleep. In the mornings she felt drained, feeling anxious and uneasy, and unable to remember what had disturbed her sleep.

Leaning wearily against the trunk of a white spruce, she watched Ebony as he walked into the stream and took a long drink. It was almost three years since Uncle Pete had spotted the magnificent stallion in a herd of wild mustangs. There was something about the horse that set him apart from the others. The herd had been rounded up and except for Ebony, the rest were sold to the Calgary Stampede, who were always looking for strong, healthy broncos. Times were tough and it was a means for the ranchers to earn extra income.

Grandpa had been against the idea of keeping Ebony from the very beginning as he felt the untrained horse would be more trouble than he was worth. However, the formidable animal demonstrated not only to be fast, but intelligent, and soon earned a reputation as a top-notch cutting horse. His one fault, which riled Grandpa to no end, was that he permitted only Pete and Caroline to ride him. The fact that he earned his keep around the ranch kept him in Grandpa's good graces.

Shivering in the bracing air, Caroline walked over to Ebony and removed her fleece-lined jacket from her pack. She put it on, grateful for the added warmth. The nasal call of a nuthatch sounded from the trees and she caught a glimpse of the tiny bird as it ran headfirst down a spruce, searching under the bark for insects.

She hoped the weather would hold for the rest of the weekend, as it was not unusual for it to snow this time of year. She spotted an osprey circling high above the crowns of the pines and watched it until it became a dark speck in the distance.

She picked up a rock and tossed it half-heartedly into the stream. A whisky jack, perched on a branch above her head, chirped saucily. Startled, Caroline realized how late it was getting. It seemed as if her mind was always wandering, and not sleeping well only added to the frustration. Grandpa had no patience with her when she neglected her chores and they often argued when he felt she was neglecting her responsibilities. Angrily, she grabbed Ebony's reins and mounted the horse.

Rather than backtrack to the main trail, covering ground she had already searched, Caroline decided to continue up the path following the brook. She urged Ebony to pick up his pace and the horse climbed steadily uphill. The path split and Caroline pulled lightly on the reins. Ebony stopped, and she rose in the stirrups and looked around, not recognizing the surroundings. She had grown up riding all the trails covering Eagle Mountain, but she did not recall having come across this fork before, and wondered if she had taken a wrong turn. She decided to turn right, as the left path appeared to head back down the mountain.

She rode for a short while, when she suddenly noticed an unpleasant odour. An elderberry bush was growing next to the path and several of its branches had been broken and crushed, and the ground around its roots had been trampled. Something had recently passed this way and Caroline hoped it was the heifer. It was getting late and she did not relish returning to the herd without it.

She steered Ebony away from the path and the nervous horse shied when he brushed against the branches. Caroline kept a tight hold on his reins. She had not ridden far when she noticed a clearing. She gently kneed Ebony forward and stopped him next to a large mountain ash.

Late Goldenrod and Yarrow, as well as dried sagebrush and thistle added to the unspoiled beauty of the meadow before her. A stream cut through the far end of the field, and to the left were the remains of a stone chimney, long since collapsed by time and weather.

All at once, her arms and legs started tingling and she felt heat radiating across her chest. Reaching inside her shirt she pulled out her locket, which had once belonged to her grandmother, and when she had died, Caroline had inherited it. The locket felt warm to her touch, but immediately cooled in the brisk air. Shrugging, she stuffed it back inside her shirt.

There was no sign of the stray, but she was so intrigued by the secreted meadow she decided to have a quick look around. She urged Ebony forward, but he refused to move, tossing his head and pulling sharply on the reins. Ebony did not shy easily and she wondered if something had frightened him.

Waiting for the big horse to settle down, she again steered him towards the open field, promising she would stop no longer than five minutes before she resumed her search for the calf.

Later, Caroline wondered if she would have made the decision she made that day if she had known how much her life was going to change.

Chapter 2
Annie and Hannah

Caroline gasped, jerking sharply on the reins. Ebony snorted and spun nervously. The collapsed chimney and vivid autumn foliage were nowhere to be seen. Before her was a neat and tidy farmhouse, surrounded by balsam poplars and white bark birch. Tulips and daffodils grew in colourful patches throughout the yard and she wondered why the flowers were in full bloom in the middle of October. The rear of the house bordered a steep slope and lilac bushes in full bloom grew down the right side of the dwelling, forming a natural barricade and providing a wind screen between the house and a red barn and a chicken coop located on the far side of the yard.

How could she have missed seeing the house and barn from the edge of the meadow? She clucked softly but Ebony nervously sidled to the left, shaking his head. Caroline applied pressure with her knees and he reluctantly obeyed, he had always been a high strung horse, but usually he did not act up when she was riding him.

Ebony trotted across the field and headed towards a dirt driveway, fighting his bit all the way. Caroline approached the farmhouse; it was painted white, had green shutters with steps leading to the front door. On the left was a covered porch, where an elderly woman sat in a rocking chair, quietly strumming a guitar. Her facc was lined with wrinkles and her silver hair was tucked inside a bonnet. She wore a flowered dress that fell below her knees and gold rimmed bifocals perched precariously on the tip of her nose. Sitting cross-legged at her feet was a young girl who looked to be around eight or nine years of age. She had long blond hair that cascaded down her back and was wearing a light blue dress and a white apron.

The old woman gestured Caroline to come forward.

"Come closer, child," she said in a raspy voice. "These ol' eyes ain't as good as they used to be."

Caroline steered Ebony to the bottom of the steps and stopped. The horse pawed the ground with his right hoof, tossing his head nervously.

"Goodness child, your horse is as skittish as a blue jay."

"Yes, ma'am. I don't know what's gotten into him, usually he's better behaved."

"Well, horses are contrary creatures, and that one looks like he has a mind of his own."

"Yes, ma'am, he does."

"Do you mind iff'in I ask your name?"

"It's Caroline Lindstrom and this is Ebony."

"Well, howdy, Caroline. Come set a spell. Names Annabelle, but folks call me Annie. This young lady is my granddaughter, Hannah."

Hannah smiled sweetly and shuffled over on the porch. Apprehensively, Caroline dismounted and tied Ebony's reins around a hitching post located in front of the porch. She walked up the creaky steps and sat down beside the obliging girl, wondering why she felt no hesitation in joining them.

Hannah shyly handed Caroline a sprig of lilacs from a bouquet she was holding in her lap. Caroline thanked her and pulled off her riding gloves, laying them on the porch.

"Our lilacs finished a long time ago," Caroline remarked, as she buried her nose in the mauve flowerets, inhaling the deep heady scent.

"You live in these here parts, Caroline?" Annie asked.

Caroline nodded. "Yes, ma'am, at the foot of Eagle Mountain, with my Grandpa and Uncle Pete."

"No cause to be so formal. You can call me Annie," she smiled, as she quietly strummed her guitar.

"How long have you lived here?" Caroline asked,

pointing at the house.

"Our family's been here since 1887."

"Wow, that's a long time. Are you the only ones farming in this area?"

"No, there are a few other homesteaders, but we don't see each other a whole lot cause of the distance."

"We have the same problem. We don't get to town very often, so I only get to see my friends in school."

Annie nodded, pushing her bifocals up higher on her nose. She leaned back in her chair and said, "Our family came from Denmark and immigrated to North Dakota in the early 1800's. They was real poor, and lived in a board-and-sod shanty. The winter of 1886 was so cold, we lost all of our cattle. In 1872 the Canadian government passed the *Dominion Lands Act* and entire families moved to Canada. There weren't nothing keeping us in North Dakota, so we come here and joined our friends and kin."

Caroline heard the pride in Annie's voice while she related her family's history.

"For ten dollars," Annie continued, "each family got one hundred and sixty acres of prime land so long as they lived on it for more'n three years, built a house and farmed thirty acres."

Caroline listened intently, vaguely remembering studying about it in school. "I think we studied that in History class, but I can't remember much about it."

"Hannah and her brother were both born in this house," Annie said.

"You know it's funny," Caroline pondered. "I've ridden all over Eagle Mountain and this is the first time I've come across this place."

"It weren't time for you to find it."

Before Caroline could ask the old woman what she meant, Annie cleared her throat and started to sing. Her voice was surprisingly clear and melodious. The song had a nostalgic subtlety about it and Caroline felt as if she had known it her whole life.

Annie sang a number of tunes and Caroline lost all track of the time. The chirping of crickets and the droning of the bees in the flowers bordering the porch created a sense of tranquillity. She took off her jacket, enjoying the unexpected pleasure of the sun's warmth.

Suddenly Annie rested her guitar against the arm of her chair. "Don't know about you two young ladies, but I'm parched. What say we go inside and make ourselves a tall pitcher of lemonade?"

"I've already stayed too long," Caroline said. "I'm looking for a missing heifer and my grandfather will wonder where I am."

"It won't take more'n a few minutes to make some," Annie commented.

"A glass of lemonade would be nice. I've been riding since early this morning."

"Come along then. I promise your granddaddy won't even know you've been gone."

The elderly woman rose slowly from her rocking chair, Hannah jumped up excitedly and followed her into the house. Caroline hesitated for a few seconds and then she opened the screen door and followed them inside. She was standing in a foyer, halfway down the hallway a flight of narrow stairs disappeared into the darkness of the second floor, and to her right was an arched doorway leading to a separate room. Caroline peeked inside as she strolled past. A stone fireplace dominated the outside wall, and an overstuffed sofa faced the hearth, an upright piano was sitting next to the window, and in the corner a huge potted fern was sitting on an oval table. The walls were papered in a colourful flower design, and a floral painting with an ornate gold frame hung on the wall above the sofa.

Caroline continued down the hallway towards the back of the house. The kitchen was warm, cozy, and smelled like cinnamon. A cast iron stove was sitting adjacent to the back wall, there was something familiar about it, and suddenly Caroline realized why. It was almost identical to the one they had at home, except this one was brand new and still had all of its original blue paint.

On the back wall, sunlight streamed through a large window that overlooked a garden. She was amazed to see green onions and peas still growing, and tomato plants just starting to flower. Except for the last of the potatoes and turnips, she had picked most of the vegetables in her garden weeks ago as it was not unusual to get frost or even snow this time of year.

"Hannah, would you mind fetchin' me the lemons from the root cellar?" Annie asked the young girl.

"Can Caroline come with me?"

"Don't' see why not, if she wants to."

Caroline nodded and followed the smiling child out the back door, and down a dirt path that led to a heavy wooden door built into the side of the hill. Hannah lifted the latch and gave it a shove, entering the dugout.

It was dark, as the outside light did not penetrate into the interior. Hannah climbed a stool and took down a kerosene lantern hanging on a hook. A small cardboard box was sitting on a shelf and she reached inside and took out a match. She struck it on the base of the lantern, lifted the glass cover, and ignited the wick.

There were wooden bins half-filled with potatoes and apples resting on the wooden shelves were rows of stewed tomatoes, pickled carrots, onions and relishes, as well as jars of jam and applesauce.

Caroline followed Hannah deeper into the root cellar. It was cool and felt refreshing after being outside in the warm air. Cobwebs hung from the earthen roof, and Caroline brushed them away from her face.

Hannah approached a large storage trunk and sitting on top was a tin canister with large sunflowers painted on it. Placing the lantern on the ground, she reached up and grabbed a small wooden box sitting on a shelf above the trunk. She opened it and took out two lemons. Caroline stared candidly at the sunflower canister, wondering why it looked so familiar.

"Granny's been saving these lemons especially for today," Hannah said, interrupting Caroline's thoughts.

Caroline was puzzled by Hannah's comment. "Are you expecting company today?"

"No silly, just you." Hannah giggled.

A shiver went down Caroline's back, how could Annie have possibly known she was coming? Before she could question Hannah further, the young girl turned and walked to the entrance of the root cellar. Wrapping her hands around the top of the lamp's chimney she blew out the flame. "I sometimes forget to blow it out," she said, looking shyly at Caroline. "Last year in the winter when it was dark, I took it with me to the chicken coop to gather eggs, and I forgot about it when I went back to the house."

"Oh, dear," Caroline said. "Did anything bad happen?"

Hannah nodded her head solemnly "One of the hens knocked it over and it started a fire. Pa saw the flames and he managed to put it out on time."

"He must have been furious with you."

"Pa hardly ever gets mad at me. He was just sad 'cause I sometimes forget about important things like that. I told him I was sorry. He told me if we had lost the chickens, we couldn't get new ones until spring."

"Where is your father?"

"Pa and my brother and our hired hand are working at one of the big ranches in the valley. They'll be gone for a while. Granny and I are taking care of the farm all by ourselves."

Caroline nodded, not finding it unusual. Often men and young boys took jobs away from their families to earn extra money. Because of the fall round-up, many of the ranches had hired on extra cowhands, the same as Grandpa had done.

When they returned to the kitchen, Hannah placed the lemons on the table. Annie had filled a pitcher with water and was dissolving sugar in it. She squeezed the lemons until she had salvaged every drop.

Caroline took the pitcher and followed Annie and Hannah outside to the porch. She noticed that Annie had set out glasses and a plate of cookies. Annie poured the lemonade and handed a glass to each of them, then she sat in her rocking chair, letting out a deep sigh.

"There's nothing better'n a glass of cold lemonade on a warm, lazy day."

It was the best lemonade Caroline had ever drunk, the sugar cookie was delicious and she helped herself to a second.

Caroline was thinking how peaceful it was sitting on the porch and that she could have stayed there forever when suddenly a squirrel chattered noisily in the tree next to the house. She flinched, realizing the shadows had lengthened and the air was beginning to cool.

"Oh, no," she said, jumping up quickly. "I've stayed too long, Grandpa will be furious."

"You better run along," Annie said. "I do thank you for dropping by, it were a real pleasure meeting you Caroline."

"I had a wonderful time and thank you for the lemonade and the cookies."

"You make sure you come back now, we sure enjoyed your company."

"Yes, ma'am, I'd like that," Caroline replied, as she grabbed her jacket and gloves. She walked quickly down the steps and over to where Ebony was patiently waiting. She stuffed her coat and gloves inside the saddle bag.

"Don't forget your lilacs," Hannah called.

"That's alright. They'll die before I get home, but

thank you anyway."

Then Caroline untied Ebony and climbed into the saddle. She raised her head to say goodbye. Annie was strumming her guitar, wistfully humming a tune, and Hannah was rearranging her bouquet of lilacs. The same feeling that Caroline had felt earlier while listening to Annie sing overcame her. Shrugging it off, she turned Ebony away from the house and trotted down the road and across the yard towards the mountain ash. She experienced the same sensation in her arms and legs as she had earlier. Ebony picked up his speed and crashed into the heavy underbrush, and again Caroline was puzzled by his reaction as he generally wasn't nervous when entering dense brush.

She had not ridden far when she started to shiver. It was definitely cooler in the trees. Retrieving her jacket and gloves, she quickly put them back on, hoping the weather wasn't taking a turn for the worse. She had Ebony pick up his pace, while the events of the day raced through her mind. Something about the whole afternoon seemed disjointed. Yet at the same time, the farm house, and the yard, and even Annie and Hannah, felt vaguely familiar.

Chapter 3
Daydreaming and a Glow in the Dark

Caroline heard her name being called in the distance. She steered Ebony towards the main trail and it was not long before she spotted Grandpa riding up the path on Riverboat, a big muscular dapple who stood over seventeen hands and could be just as cantankerous as his owner. She hoped Grandpa had not been looking for her all the time she was gone. He would have every right to be angry with her, and she knew he would not be happy she had stopped to visit with strangers when she should have been looking for the heifer.

"Caroline, there you are," he said, stopping Riverboat a few feet away from Ebony. "We found the stray."

"I'm sorry I was gone so long, Grandpa, but I decided to look higher up the trail."

"Well you couldn't have ridden very far, you've only been gone for a few minutes."

Caroline looked uncomfortably at Grandpa, but did not respond to his remark. Perhaps in the confusion of trying to find the stray, he had not realized how much time had passed.

She was just about to tell him about meeting Annie and Hannah, when Grandpa turned Riverboat around and urged the horse to pick up his pace. "Come along, Caroline," he said, turning in his saddle to look at her. "We have a long ride ahead of us and I want to get home before it gets dark."

With the commotion in herding the cattle down the mountain, and later currying and feeding Ebony, Caroline's encounter with Annie completely slipped her mind. Rather than stoke up the wood stove, they ate cold beef sandwiches and potato salad for supper. By the time

Caroline had cleaned up the kitchen, she barely had enough energy to climb the stairs to the second floor. As she passed the mirror hanging in the hallway, she quickly glanced at her reflection. Her braids fell past her shoulders, she was pale and there were dark shadows under her eyes. She always thought her blond hair and blue eyes were so ordinary, and silently wished she looked like Suzanne Chalmers, her best friend, whose jet black hair and dark eyes gave her an exotic look. Over the past year, Suzanne had grown taller and had filled out, while Caroline, who had always been small-boned and slender, had not changed at all.

She closed her bedroom door, dropped her backpack on the floor and flung herself across her bed. It was covered by a patchwork quilt her grandmother had made for her when she was very young and Caroline cherished it.

Thinking of Suzanne brought up a flood of unwanted memories. School was out for the long Thanksgiving weekend and they had planned to meet at the bus stop to talk before Caroline's bus arrived. Suzanne's fifteenth birthday was on Saturday and she was putting on her first mixed party. It was all she had talked about for the past three weeks. When Suzanne joined her, Caroline had interrupted her as soon as she had begun talking, confessing she would not be coming to the party.

At first Suzanne had stared at her in disbelief. "You're joking?" she had said, laughing uneasily.

"I'm sorry, Suzanne," Caroline had replied staring unhappily at the ground.

"It's your grandpa, isn't it? Did you try to explain to him it's a mixed party, and it's chaperoned?"

Coming from a close-knit family, Suzanne had never understood why Caroline had such a volatile relationship with her grandfather. Over time, Caroline had stopped trying to explain how unreasonable Grandpa could be. Both of them had short tempers and more often than not their discussions ended up in shouting matches.

"I know I should have said something earlier, but you were so excited, and I didn't know how to bring it up without hurting your feelings."

"I can't believe you're doing this," Suzanne had yelled, her black eyes glaring. "You're supposed to be my best friend, but I guess I was wrong."

The hurtful words made Caroline feel even worse. She had reached over and placed her hand on Suzanne's arm, hoping to calm her enough so she could explain, but Suzanne had angrily shaken it off.

It was then that Suzanne's mother had driven up. Mrs. Chalmers had waved at the two girls, unaware that they had just exchanged heated words.

"I have to go. Mom is driving me to Olds to buy me a poodle skirt for my birthday," Suzanne said. "Not that you care, since you had no intention of coming to my party anyway."

Suzanne had then jumped into the front seat and rolled up the window; Caroline had watched wretchedly as the car had driven away.

Caroline rolled over and stared at the wall, angrily pulling the quilt up under her chin. She had not been entirely truthful with Suzanne, who had assumed she had talked to Grandpa about the party. In truth, Caroline had not discussed the matter with him until later that evening. Grandpa had been quiet during supper, Pete had finished eating, had stood up and left the kitchen, muttering he had some last minute chores to attend to before it got dark. Grandpa had walked over to the stove and poured himself a second cup of coffee. He returned to the table, picked up his newspaper and began reading. "You want to tell me why you were late getting home again?" he asked angrily.

"I…I, guess I lost track of time. I'm sorry," Caroline had stammered, taken unawares by his abruptness.

"The school bus drops you off at the end of our driveway, which is only a few minutes away from the front door. If you spent less time daydreaming and more time tending to your chores, then I wouldn't have to keep after you all the time."

"I decided to walk through the woods. I wanted some time to myself before I got into this house."

"I don't need your sarcastic remarks, young lady. You have responsibilities, the same as everyone else around here does, and..."

"I know all that," Caroline interrupted rudely. "But I was upset because of Suzanne's party."

"Who's Suzanne?" Grandpa asked, shaking his head, a puzzled look on his face.

"Suzanne Chalmers, she's my friend from school."

"She Grant and Sharon's girl?"

Caroline nodded. "Suzanne's birthday is tomorrow and she's putting on a party this weekend and she asked me if I wanted to go."

Grandpa slowly folded the paper and placed it on the table.

"It's going to be chaperoned and you know Mr. and Mrs. Chalmers," Caroline had said, knowing full well she should have let the matter drop.

"I haven't seen the Chalmers in years," Grandpa grunted.

"All of my friends will be there."

"That still doesn't make it right. You're far too young to be going to a party where there will be a bunch of boys."

"I'm going on fifteen," Caroline had answered angrily. "Kids my age go to mixed parties all the time. They're even dating and going to the movies together." Too late, she realized she had overstepped her boundaries.

"How many times have we had this discussion?" Grandpa yelled, slamming his fist down on the table.

"That's the end of the matter, Caroline, the answer is no."

Caroline stared down at her plate. "Don't worry, I knew what your answer would be, so I already told Suzanne I wouldn't be going."

"I don't know why you're going on about some party this weekend anyway. You haven't forgotten its fall round up and we leave for Eagle Mountain first thing in the morning?"

"I forgot all about it," Caroline gasped, raising her head.

"I figured as much. After you finish cleaning up these dishes, you better go upstairs and pack, unless you want to stay home by yourself this year."

Caroline jumped up and began clearing the table. How could she have forgotten? Angrily, she realized her argument with Suzanne wouldn't have happened at all if she had been honest and had told her right away the party was the same weekend as the fall round-up.

When the kitchen was in order, she had raced upstairs to her bedroom. Herding the cattle down the mountain usually took no more than a day, but sometimes the weather took a turn for the worst, and there was always the possibility of having to spend the night on the mountain. It was always smart to bring extra clothing, especially gloves and socks.

She had not regretted her outburst when she told Grandpa many kids her age were dating because she was used to his archaic ideas on that topic. What bothered her was lying to Suzanne and her friends every time she was asked to join them in town. She would have been mortified to tell them her grandfather thought she was too young to attend parties, especially if there were boys invited.

Exhausted as she was, it took her a long time to fall asleep and the last thing she remembered was the soft strumming of a guitar and the scent of lilacs.

The next morning Caroline overslept. She hastily

threw on a pair of old jeans and a plaid shirt. Grandpa had begrudgingly agreed to let her wear jeans as long as she was doing chores around the ranch. Maybe one day, girls would be able to wear pants and shirts to school, but she doubted if that would ever happen. Even though it was 1955, you'd have thought they were living in the Dark Ages.

She looked out the window and spotted Grandpa, Pete, Frank Gilroy and Lucas Jones, the two cowhands Grandpa had hired, at work in the corral.

Groaning, she raced down the stairs. The stove was not lit, which meant there was no coffee for the men, and breakfast had not been started. The kitchen was chilly and she rubbed her hands together to warm them up.

She stared at the old wood stove, most of its original blue colour had worn away, and no matter how often she scrubbed it, she could not get rid of the black soot imbedded deeply in the cast iron. She had always hated it and struggled with it every time she tried to light it. Enviously, she thought of the brand-new stove in Annie's kitchen.

She grabbed a handful of old newspapers and wood from the wood box. Returning to the stove, she checked the direct draft to the chimney and the slide at the base of the smoke pipe. After grappling with it for a few seconds, she finally managed to open the damper. Scrunching up the paper, she lifted the front burner and stuffed it inside, along with some kindling, and tossed in a couple of lit matches. She threw in several pieces of wood and soon the fire was burning briskly. She waited until the flames were hot before she closed the damper.

The first thing Caroline did was make coffee. Grandpa insisted that a full pot be kept on the back burner all the time and he would not have been happy that it wasn't ready this morning. She sighed, as she was in no mood to have a heated discussion with him about it and hoped he would let it pass.

She walked towards the back of the kitchen and opened a heavy wooden door. Steps led downwards into the darkness. Walking carefully, she placed her hand on the wall for support. Arriving at the bottom, she reached up and pulled a chain hanging from the ceiling, a light came on, but it was so dim it was hard to see into the far corners.

The area was not much more than a dugout, the ceiling and the walls were supported by two-by-four planks, and the floor was dirt. Wooden shelves had been built along the right hand side. The room was always cool and made a perfect place for storing their food and preserves.

Grandpa never tired of telling how his father had designed and built the room under the house, providing them with an indoor root cellar, allowing them the comfort of not having to go outside, especially during the winter. Caroline never understood Grandpa's pride in the root cellar, as most people had refrigerators now and root cellars were rapidly disappearing.

A large wooden bin full of potatoes dominated a large portion of the space. Separate wooden containers filled with carrots, turnips and beets surrounded the bin, and mason jars holding fruit, tomatoes, relishes and pickles canned by Caroline filled the shelves. She recalled Annie's cellar and the half-empty vegetable bins.

A glass bowl filled with eggs and covered with a kitchen towel was sitting on the bottom shelf. She was glad she had gathered eggs after school on Friday, as it saved her from having to collect them this morning before breakfast. Then she grabbed a basket and filled it with potatoes, carrots and turnips, as she planned to make a beef stew for supper. It was filling and there wouldn't be as many dishes to wash afterwards.

As she turned to leave, Caroline heard a soft rustling sound. She spun around, catching the bowl of eggs before it crashed to the floor. A dull glow emanating from the far side of the room caught the corner of her eye. She seldom went over there as it was musty and overrun with spiders. Just as quickly as it had appeared, the light disappeared. Caroline shrugged, turned and headed towards the steps. She had probably heard a mouse and the gleam was more than likely a reflection of the light bulb on a metal object.

Quickly grabbing her coat, she ran out the back door and headed towards the smoke house. She grabbed a rafter of bacon and a small roast, and returned to the kitchen.

Soon breakfast was ready, and Caroline stepped outside. She struck a metal triangle hanging from the porch eave with the striker. She startled a flock of cedar waxwings eating fermented crab apples in a tree growing next to the porch.

She watched the four men as they walked towards the house.

Two men couldn't have been more different than Grandpa and Pete. Grandpa was a very large man, well over six feet, with grey hair that fell to his shoulders, and angry blue eyes. His disposition was severe and brooding and he seldom smiled or laughed.

Pete Morgan, or Uncle Pete as Caroline called him, had lived with Grandpa since he was a young boy. He was long-limbed and reedy, with a dark weathered face, high cheekbones and eyes as black as midnight, validating his Native heritage. He walked with a limp from an injury he had received as a young man competing in a bareback riding contest at one of the local rodeos. He had also ridden as an Outrider in the Chuck Wagon Races at the Calgary Stampede, yet whenever Caroline asked him about his leg, he always evaded answering her. She sensed it was something he did not want to discuss, so she never pressured him about it. He seldom talked, but when he did he spoke softly and easily, he lived alone in the bunk house and came and went as he pleased.

Caroline returned to the kitchen and scooped hot water out of the stove reservoir. Returning to the coat room, she filled a metal basin sitting on top of a small table.

It wasn't long before she heard footsteps on the porch. The screen door opened and closed with a sharp bang. Grandpa commanded Rusty to stay outside on the porch. Rusty was their mixed Collie-German Shepherd, and although he was not allowed inside the house, he never stopped trying. When the weather went below freezing, he was permitted to sleep in the coat room, or more often than not, he slept with Pete in the bunkhouse. Grandpa did not believe in pampering any of the animals living at the ranch. They each had a role to play. Rusty's job was to chase away wild animals that wandered too close to the chicken coop or to warn them in the house if bears or cougars came too close to the livestock, especially the horses in the barn.

The men entered the kitchen, their hair slicked back and their hands and faces scrubbed clean. Caroline laid platters of eggs, bacon, fried potatoes, and toast on the table and kept their cups full of hot coffee. When everyone had eaten and the men had returned to work, she filled the sink with water from the hand pump. After pouring ladles of hot water from the stove reservoir into the sink, it was warm enough to wash the dishes. She had always hated this chore, and not for the hundredth time, wished they had indoor plumbing.

She remembered when Grandpa had finally given in and had electricity installed in the house. When she suggested the old wood stove be converted over, he told her that it cooked just as well as an electric stove, and it provided enough heat, along with the wood burning fireplace in the living room to keep the whole house warm during the winter. There was no need in wasting good money.

It had taken her a long time to convince Grandpa they should have a telephone. He argued with her for months, convinced the cost of having it installed was more than they could afford. She tried to tell him that if they went on a party line, it was not that expensive, and if there was ever an emergency, having a telephone in the house was a good idea. When he missed a very important meeting with The Western Stock Growers Association in town because none of the members had time to drive out to the ranch to let him know about it, he finally gave in.

Caroline knew people were struggling financially as it was only ten years since the War, and there weren't very many jobs available. Grandpa always said they were luckier than most families, as they grew and raised all of their own food, and as the ranch had been in the family for over fifty years they did not have mortgage payments to worry about. Money was scarce, and deep down Caroline knew they could not afford luxuries such as in-door plumbing and gas furnaces. But it still did not stop her in wishing for them.

Before returning to the corral, Grandpa had mentioned one of the calves had a deep cut on its leg, and had asked Caroline to call the area veterinarian, Dr. Redding, to see if he could drive out and have a look at it. Caroline did not have to be told to invite the doctor to stay for supper, as it was a long drive out to the ranch.

She quickly made baking soda biscuits to go with the stew. Later, during supper, Caroline apologized because there was no butter. Dr. Redding merely shrugged, and took a second biscuit, complimenting her on the meal. Families were struggling to survive and he was often paid for his services in fresh produce or meat. He always got a laugh when he said the same thing every time. "Now a single fellow living on his own would have to be crazy to turn down a delicious home-cooked meal like this, pass the spuds."

The two hired cowhands would be staying overnight in the bunk house with Pete. In the morning, the three of them would herd the cattle to a rendezvous point, and then they, along with a number of other ranchers from the area, would herd the steers to Olds. They would be taken to the Canadian Pacific Railway freight yards and delivered to a slaughter house in Calgary. Olds was only thirty miles away and it would not take the herders more than two days for the round trip. Some of the larger ranches in the area, like their neighbours, the Mitchells, transported their beef by truck, but the smaller ranch owners could not afford to rent them. Grandpa would remain at the ranch and Caroline would help him do Pete's chores.

The next day, after Pete and the cowhands had left, Caroline picked the last of the potatoes, carrots, beets and turnips, topping up the bins in the root cellar. Then she canned over a dozen jars of relishes. She loved doing the gardening and the preserving, but it was a lot of work, and she sometimes wished she had more help. She, Grandpa and Pete were the only ones living at the ranch. Her parents had died when she was very young. Her father had moved to Red Deer a few years after graduating from high school, he had wanted to modernize the ranch, but Grandpa had refused to make any changes, and they had quarrelled.

Her father had met her mother, then Elizabeth O'Hara, and they had married in 1937. World War II broke out, and Caroline was born in 1941. Unfortunately, her mother did not survive her birth and her father was left with an infant to bring up on his own.

Her father enlisted in the Canadian Army in 1942 and in 1943, he was shipped overseas and Caroline came to live with her grandparents at Eagle Ridge Ranch. Just a few days before the War ended, the family received a telegram. Robert Lindstrom had been killed in action in Germany while heroically defending his country, and not long after receiving the telegram, a package arrived with his personal effects, and then later his medals and commendations. Her father and Grandpa had never reconciled, Caroline was only four years old at the time, and because there were no pictures anywhere in the house of her parents, her father's face was a distant memory.

Grandma Lindstrom took over the role of both mother and grandmother and Caroline loved her dearly. She had a passion and love for the Alberta foothills and passed her pride and knowledge on to her granddaughter. They would spend hours riding and hiking over the numerous mountain trails. Grandma would tell Caroline the names of the plants, bushes and wildflowers and teach her the habits of the animals and the birds. Caroline was twelve years old when Grandma came down with influenza and died unexpectedly. Her death created a void not only in Caroline's heart, but in Grandpa's as well. He became even more withdrawn and sullen, and it was a very confusing time in her life. If it hadn't been for Pete, Caroline was not sure if she would have been able to cope. He never interfered with the way Grandpa disciplined her, but she sensed he did not always agree with his decisions.

The day passed quickly and that evening after supper, she toyed with the idea of telling Grandpa about Annie and Hannah, yet something stopped her from bringing the matter up. She did wonder, however, why Grandpa had never mentioned the fact there were homesteaders farming on Eagle Mountain, especially since he claimed to know every square inch of the mountain.

Chapter 4
Lonesome Checkers and Financial Woes

Caroline was up early the next morning. When her chores were done, she grabbed her lunch pail and hurried down the driveway towards the main road.

The bunk house door opened and Rusty came charging out. When he spotted Caroline, he raced over to her and jumped up on her clean dress, snagging her wool sweater with his nails. She scratched him behind his ears, then ordered the enthusiastic dog to get down.

She wiped the dirt off her dress, looking casually around the yard. The driveway led to a two story log house, which boasted a covered porch that wrapped around the entire structure. Two rocking chairs and a small wicker seat were located halfway between the front door and a large picture window. The house was over fifty year's old and needed repairs inside and out. The wooden shakes on the roof were curling and needed to be replaced, the porch steps had started to buckle and half of the railings were missing.

To the right of the house, next to the trees, was a dilapidated barn weathered by the elements. A portion of its roof had collapsed long ago and was propped up by a lodge pole pine. Attached to the barn was a corral with a cattle chute that funnelled into a large fenced pasture.

Scattered around the yard were a number of outbuildings; a tool shed where Grandpa's ancient John Deere tractor was stored; a chicken coop and the ramshackle bunk house where Pete lived.

When she arrived at the main gate, Caroline fleetingly glanced at the sign hanging by a single rusty nail, swinging forlornly in the light breeze. The words "Eagle Ridge Ranch" had been painted on it in bold letters, but over the years had faded into the bleached wood.

It was not long before the school bus arrived. Caroline boarded, and greeted the driver, Mr. Olson.

A stocky boy with sandy hair and freckles was sitting in the last row and he waved when he spotted her. Caroline strolled down the aisle and sat in the seat next to him. Wesley Mitchell and Caroline had known each other all their lives. They lived approximately twenty miles west of the town of Sundre, which is where they attended school. Wesley's dad owned the Double M Ranch, one of the largest and most influential ranches in the area.

"I didn't see you at Suzanne's party on Saturday," he said, clearing his throat.

Caroline stared out the window. "I couldn't make it."

"Yeah, I heard you and Suzanne talking at the bus stop on Friday."

"I imagine the whole school heard us."

Wesley chuckled. "You know Scott was at the party."

"I know."

"The only reason he went was because he thought you were going. He really likes you."

Caroline blushed. She lowered her eyes and stared despondently at her lap. "I hope he isn't angry at me."

"He was a bit disappointed at first, but I explained to him why you couldn't come."

"What did you tell him?"

"That your grandfather wasn't exactly the easiest person in the world to live with. I also reminded him about the round-up and he understood why you couldn't make it."

"Thanks, Wesley."

"I guess I've known your grandfather long enough to know it wouldn't have done you any good to ask him anyways. Don't worry about Suzanne, she won't stay mad long. She has a short fuse, but she'll get over it."

Caroline knew that Wesley liked Suzanne, although

her friend hadn't figured it out yet.

Scott was Suzanne's older brother, and Wesley was his best friend. Even though they were both in grade eleven, and Caroline and Suzanne were two grades below them, the two boys, as well as a few of their friends, had agreed to come to the party. Normally they wouldn't have been caught dead going to a party put on by someone in the ninth grade, but Caroline realized the only reason Scott had gone was because of her. Wesley reminding her did not make her feel any better, but she realized he was only being kind.

The old bus laboured down the rutted dirt road, its engine grinding in protest. The dense trees gradually lessened, and soon they were passing wheat fields and small farms. In the background, Caroline could see Eagle Mountain rising high above the dark rolling hills. To her there was no place more beautiful than the Alberta foothills.

Wesley and Caroline sat quietly, comfortable in their silence. Finally they arrived at the school. Suzanne and Scott were waiting for them at the bus stop. Before Caroline could say anything to either of them, the school bell rang and everyone rushed to their classrooms.

Suzanne seemed to have forgotten all about their disagreement. When they were seated at their desks, she leaned over and whispered in Caroline's ear. "I have something really cool to tell you."

Before Caroline could ask her what it was, their teacher tapped her chalk on the board and everyone quieted down.

While walking to their next class, Suzanne pulled Caroline aside and said. "I danced three times with Wesley."

"Like, wow. Do you think he's hip?"

"Wesley, a hipster, not really, but he's really nice."

"Yes, he is," Caroline chuckled.

The two girls strolled casually down the hallway. Suddenly, Suzanne turned and faced Caroline. "Scott was pretty frosted when you didn't show up."

"I know and I'm really sorry. It's just as well, because I had completely forgotten about fall round-up. We spent the whole day on Eagle Mountain rounding up the calves, so I couldn't have gotten away even if I wanted to. I hope you and Scott can forgive me?"

"Of course I do. Don't worry about Scott. You know how laid-back he is, and he never goes ape about anything. When Wesley reminded him about the round-up, he understood completely."

"Come along girls, you're going to be late for your next class," Caroline and Suzanne started when Mr. Golden, the vice-principal interrupted them. They quickly apologized then headed down the hallway.

Caroline happily mulled over what Suzanne had just told her. The next time she spoke to Scott, she would have to pretend she didn't know how he felt about her, and would wait for him to make the first move.

Caroline was in her bedroom that night doing her homework when she suddenly started thinking about Annie and Hannah. It seemed as if they were always in her thoughts. She decided it would be a good time to ask Grandpa about them and maybe he would be able to answer some of her questions.

She wandered downstairs to the living room. There was a fire burning in the large stone fireplace. Grandpa was reading a book and Pete was playing a game of Lonesome Checkers. Caroline smiled at him when he muttered quietly under his breath and then moved one of the pieces to a red square. When he couldn't get anyone to play a game with him, Pete would play alone, which is how he came up with the name Lonesome Checkers. When Caroline asked him how he knew who won, he would tell her he always did, because there wasn't anyone in a hundred miles smart enough to beat him.

"Grandpa," Caroline asked as she walked over to where he was sitting. "When I was looking for the stray calf on Saturday, I came across a fork on the path up by the ridge, and it led to a large meadow. I've never seen it before and I wondered if you knew anything about it?"

Grandpa laid down his book and looked up at Caroline. "There were a few homesteads up in that area, but that was years ago. They're all gone now. There's nothing left but trees and bush."

"But I saw an old crumbled chimney and there was a brook on the far side of the field."

Grandpa shook his head irritably. "Caroline, I've spent my entire life here, and I know every square inch of Eagle Mountain. There isn't a meadow anywhere near where you were."

"But that's not all I saw, I..."

"That's enough, Caroline. You better get ready for bed, five o'clock comes early."

Not wanting to rile him any further, Caroline let the matter drop. She had started to tell him about meeting Annie and Hannah, but for some reason she stopped. Instinctively, she knew that now was not the time to say anything.

She strolled over and stood behind Pete, watching him play with his imaginary opponent. "Are you winning, Uncle Pete?"

"Afraid so, sometimes it's meddlesome being so darn smart."

Caroline grinned and patted Pete on his shoulder. She walked towards the hallway and noticed from the corner of her eye Pete and Grandpa exchanging glances. When Grandpa saw her watching him, he quickly picked up his book.

She headed to the coat room, put on her jacket, and went outside. It was a cold, clear night, and the distant hooting of an owl added an eeriness to the stillness. She strolled around to the front of the house and leaned on the precarious railing. Rusty had climbed up on the wicker lounge to sleep, and when he heard her, he jumped down and walked over to where she was standing. He leaned against her legs and Caroline reached down and scratched him under his chin. She murmured quietly to the old dog and he wagged his tail happily, enjoying the attention.

The stars were so bright, Caroline felt as if she could reach up and pluck them from the sky. A brilliant harvest moon shone through the branches of the poplars and aspens. Sighing, she entered through the front door, passed the living room and headed towards the stairs.

Suddenly, she heard her name being mentioned. She stopped on the bottom step.

"You can't be serious," she heard Pete say. "There has to be some other way."

"If you think of any, then maybe you could let me know," Grandpa responded, a hint of anger in his voice. "Unless I get some money soon, we're going to lose the ranch. I won't be able to pay next year's taxes and I've been running on a debit at the feed lot for months."

"But selling Ebony would kill her. Look, I have a little money saved..."

"I don't want your charity, Pete," Grandpa interrupted. "This is my problem, not yours."

"Still look at me as being a hired hand after all these years, Joseph?"

"Don't talk such nonsense. You're a member of this family and always will be."

"Then let me help you out."

"Pete, I know what kind of a salary you make, and what you've saved won't make a dent on what I owe. Leonard Mitchell has offered me a lot of money for that horse. He knows Ebony is the fastest and smartest cutting horse in Alberta and I may have no choice but to take him up on his offer."

"Mitchell can buy ten quarter horses. Why would he want to buy Ebony?"

"That's not the reason why he wants him. He's quite aware of how hard Ebony is to handle. He wants him as a stud. Leonard's been talking about breeding quarter horses for years and he feels there's a market for it."

"Sounds like you've discussed this at length and you've already made up your mind?"

"This ranch has been in the family for over fifty years and I don't plan on losing it."

"How soon does Mitchell need your answer?"

"Not right away, I guess. He says it's an open offer. But I can't wait forever, Pete. I have to let him know what my decision is fairly soon."

"Can we make it through the winter?"

"I believe so. The sale of the heifers will get us through until spring and if we tighten our belts, we should be okay until then."

"Hold off as long as you can before you give Mitchell your answer. Maybe something will happen and things will work themselves out."

"I don't believe in miracles, Pete."

"I'm not expecting a miracle, but sometimes fate has a way of intervening."

"I've never known you to be such an optimist."

"No harm in hoping. Don't say anything to Caroline about this. She doesn't need to know and worrying about it all winter won't do her any good."

"Pete, I don't want to do this anymore than you do, but right now it's our only solution."

"I know, Joseph. Life can be pretty unfair at times."

Grandpa grunted, but did not respond.

Realizing she would be seen, Caroline quickly hid under the stairwell, just seconds before Pete appeared in the hallway. He walked towards the front door and then suddenly stopped. Turning, he stared directly at where she was hiding. Caroline crouched tightly against the wall, hiding in the shadows. He opened the door and left.

Caroline stood up and peeked around the corner. Seeing the way was clear, she quietly climbed the stairs. When she got to her room, she sat numbly on the edge of her bed. Putting on her pyjamas she crawled under the quilt, curling into a tight ball.

Grandpa was right, five o'clock did come early.

Chapter 5
Golden Haired Angel and a Silver Broach

The weather turned colder and the first snow fell in early December. Caroline loved watching the gently falling flakes. The branches of the firs and spruce trees were soon covered in a blanket of white. Grandpa complained about the cold, she knew he was worried his old tractor and plough would not make it through the winter. Keeping the driveway cleared was a full time job.

Pete and Grandpa spent hours every day chopping wood and Caroline's job was to make sure the bins in the living room and kitchen were kept full. At times, there was a heavy snowfall during the night, and the school bus couldn't get through. On those days, Caroline had to stay home and as there was never a shortage of chores, she kept herself busy.

Over the long winter months, her thoughts turned often to Annie, usually just before she fell asleep, and she could not understand why she was so preoccupied with the elderly woman. Often she woke in the mornings, exhausted and anxious, knowing she had been dreaming again, yet unable to remember what she had dreamed about. Whenever she entered the root cellar, a sense of apprehension would overtake her, and she would quickly grab what she wanted and leave. The corner where she had first seen the dull light seemed to beckon to her and Caroline made a point of steering clear of it.

Christmas arrived and school was out for the holiday. Caroline had spotted the perfect fir tree earlier in the year not far from the barn. She told Pete about it, and two days before Christmas, they bundled up warmly and headed into the trees. Water trickled under the snow, as a Chinook wind had arrived a few days earlier and was rapidly melting the snow and ice. The weather was always so unpredictable in Alberta. One year it would be one blizzard after another and the next there might not be any snow until the end of December. Caroline loved the diversity in the weather, although Grandpa and Pete complained that it was difficult to figure out what the next hour would bring, let alone the next day.

Caroline pointed out the tree and Pete quickly chopped it down. Soon they were trudging through the snow, laughing and talking on their way back to the house. They set the tree up in the living room next to the fireplace and Caroline spent hours decorating it. The ornaments were getting old, but she wouldn't have replaced them for anything, as each one held a special memory.

On Christmas Eve, they dressed in their best clothes and drove to Sundre to attend midnight mass. Last year there had been a blizzard and they couldn't get through the drifts. This year, because of the timely Chinook, the road was passable, and Grandpa was able to drive his old Ford pickup all the way through.

When they arrived at the church, Caroline spotted the Chalmers driving into the parking lot. "Grandpa, can I go over and say hi to Suzanne?"

Grandpa nodded distractedly at Caroline. He had spotted Mr. Mitchell talking with a small group of men. All of them were active members of The Western Stock Growers Association and Caroline knew they would soon be talking about the price of beef, which seemed to be the main topic discussed whenever the farmers and ranchers got together. Caroline did not think Mr. Mitchell would bring up the matter of buying Ebony in front of the other ranchers, and since Grandpa had promised Pete he would wait until spring before giving Mr. Mitchell his decision, she knew he would honour his end of the bargain.

Caroline spotted Pete talking to a few of his friends on the far side of the parking lot. One of them said something and Pete shook his head and laughed. Most of his friends were cowhands hired on at the larger ranches, or drifting from place to place looking for any kind of work available. It was not often they got a chance to get together and visit.

She walked over to where the Chalmers had parked their car. Mr. Chalmers was laughing at Mrs. Chalmers, who was chasing Teddy and Charlie, their six year old twins around the churchyard, trying to get them to settle down. They were known by everyone in the Chalmers family as the Terrible Twosome and Caroline thought the label suited them perfectly.

Suzanne waved and Caroline ran over to join her.

"Oh, Caroline, I'm so glad you made it. Can you sit with me?"

"I don't know. I'll go ask Grandpa."

"Okay, I'll come with you."

Caroline walked over to Grandpa and waited while he talked to Mr. Mitchell.

"Something wrong, Caroline?" he asked, when he suddenly noticed her waiting.

"No, sir. I was wondering if I could sit with Suzanne in church."

Grandpa nodded, "Just make sure you come to the truck as soon as mass is over, we have a long drive ahead of us. Pete says there's going to be a change in the weather and you know he's never wrong."

"Thanks, Grandpa," Caroline replied. She and Suzanne linked arms and strolled towards the church. Scott saw them and walked over to join them. Wesley Mitchell was with him.

"Hi, Caroline," Scott said.

"Hi," Caroline said, her face turning a deep pink. Thank goodness it was dark outside and Scott didn't notice her blushing.

"Come on," Suzanne said. "Let's find a place to sit before Mom and Dad and the Terrible Twosome decide to join us."

The four friends sat together near the back, talking quietly until the service started. Caroline loved going to midnight mass and she listened contentedly as the choir's melodic voices reverberated throughout the nave. The songs were in Latin and Caroline sang the words quietly to herself. She quietly said a prayer, hoping that Mr. Mitchell would change his mind and decide against buying Ebony.

All too soon, the service was over and Caroline had to say goodbye. The four friends stood by the back entrance, waiting for the church to empty. Suzanne reached inside her pocket and handed Caroline a small package. "Merry Christmas, Caroline."

"But I didn't bring anything for you."

"That's okay. Christmas is for giving, not receiving, remember? Besides, it reminded me of you."

Caroline gave her friend a hug.

"There's something in there from me as well," Scott said. "I thought it would be easier putting it in the same package."

Caroline looked shyly at Scott and nodded her thanks. He was grinning from ear to ear.

"I have to go. Grandpa's waiting at the truck. Have a wonderful Christmas, everyone."

Caroline raced out of the church and over to the parking lot. Grandpa was sitting in the cab of the truck and she knew he would be cursing and muttering under his breath as the old heater blasted out cold air. She climbed inside and pulled her coat collar up to keep her ears warm. Pete opened the passenger door, reached behind the seat for the ice scraper and started cleaning the front window. Pete's prediction in a turn of the weather was accurate, as always, and Caroline hoped it wouldn't start snowing before they got home.

She reached inside her pocket and grabbed the gift, holding it tightly.

After a couple of stalls and a few pushes from Pete to get the truck started again, they finally arrived safely at home.

When she was by herself in her room, Caroline turned on the lamp and sat in the middle of her bed, staring at the brightly wrapped package. She unwrap the beautiful Christmas paper, being careful not to tear it. There were two little boxes inside. One of them had her name on it and she recognized Suzanne's flowery handwriting. Caroline opened it and inside was a Christmas ornament for the tree. It was a small angel with blond hair and a glittering halo. She knew the perfect spot to put it. The second box was smaller. Inside was a beautiful silver broach. It was a horse and its right front leg was raised. Caroline had never seen anything so lovely. She pinned it on her dress, admiring the way it looked. Then she lay down on her bed and stared dreamily at the ceiling.

"Caroline, are you still up?" Grandpa called from down the hall.

Startled, Caroline sat up quickly, pushing her hair away from her face. She jumped off the bed and opened her bedroom door. "Yes, Grandpa," she said, gasping to catch her breath. "I'm just putting out the light."

"You better get some sleep. We still have to get up at five o'clock. The chores won't do themselves."

"Good night, Grandpa," she said as she closed her door.

Knowing that he must never see the broach, she removed it and hid it in the back of her jewellery box.

Then she quickly put on her pyjamas and jumped into bed. The room was cold and Caroline could see her breath. Snuggling deep into Grandma's quilt, she closed her eyes.

This was the best Christmas she had ever had.

Chapter 6
A Second Visit and a Bouquet of Lilacs

Each morning, Caroline took the broach out of her jewellery box and hid it in her lunch pail. She would pin it on her sweater at her locker, so that it was the first thing Scott would see. Caroline never mentioned Scott to Grandpa or Pete, although she did talk about Suzanne periodically.

Time went by quickly and she anxiously waited for spring thaw. Annie was in her thoughts constantly and although Caroline could not understand why she felt compelled to do so, she knew she had to return to the meadow. The trails on Eagle Mountain would not be passable and there was no way she could get through during the winter.

Spring arrived and the snow began melting. Her chance finally came in late April. Grandpa announced he was going to meet Mr. Mitchell and some of the other ranchers in town, as a special meeting of the Western Stock Growers Association had been called. He would be gone for most of the day. As soon as his pickup disappeared down the roadway, Caroline raced to the barn and into Ebony's stall. She quickly saddled him and led him outside. The sun had appeared about an hour before. It was a perfect day to go riding.

Pete was working in the corral, shoeing one of the horses, his back facing the barn door. Caroline jumped onto Ebony's back, shouting that she was going riding as she galloped past him. He waved at her without turning around.

Caroline trotted Ebony down the roadway and turned onto the trail heading towards Eagle Mountain. She pulled her cowboy hat down so that its brim shadowed her face. Although it was still early spring, her fair skin burned easily. She let her thoughts wander, enjoying the warmth of the sun. There were pockets of snow lying in the shadows of the trees, under rocky overhangs, and along the banks of the stream. Sprigs of new growth poked through the earth and the sweet scent of the fir trees filled the air.

The higher they climbed, the cooler it became. Caroline put on her denim jacket, and pulled on her leather gloves, glad she had remembered to pack them.

A curious whisky jack followed them from tree to tree, chirping his indignation at their intrusion. Caroline talked to the saucy bird and laughed when it turned its head sideways, almost as if it understood what she was saying.

She stayed on the main trail, climbing steadily upwards. She spotted a delicate trillium growing under a fallen log, the first flower she had seen this spring. An hour passed and she arrived at the fork. She turned right and followed the winding trail upwards. She was sure this was where she had ridden last fall, yet she did not recognize any of the landmarks. Just when she was ready to turn Ebony around, she spotted a patch of green shimmering through the tightly packed trees. She steered Ebony away from the trail and there before them was the mountain ash. Once again she felt the tingling in her arms and legs and as had happened before Ebony reared and tossed his head when Caroline urged him forward. She could not see anything that might make him nervous and she remembered Annie's words about horses being contrary.

Nothing had changed and surprisingly, the lilac bushes and the tulips and daffodils were once again in full bloom. The weather patterns were definitely different here and Caroline decided to ask Annie why that was the case.

She approached the house, jumped down from Ebony's back, and wrapped his reins around the hitching post. She chuckled to herself, as she was half expecting to see Annie and Hannah on the porch exactly where they were when she last saw them. There was no one in sight, she climbed the steps and approached the front door. "Hello is anyone home?" she called.

She heard footsteps inside the house and suddenly the door was flung open. It was Hannah and when she saw Caroline, a surprised look crossed her face. "Hi, Caroline. How come you're back so soon?"

Caroline stared at the young girl in bemusement, not quite sure how to answer her question. She tousled the top of Hannah's head and said hesitantly. "I missed you so much I couldn't stay away."

Hannah giggled and shrugged her shoulders shyly.

"Is your grandma around, Hannah?"

Without responding, Hannah spun around and raced down the hallway, leaving Caroline alone on the porch.

"Granny, it's Caroline, she's back again."

"Well, for land sakes, child, ask her to come in," a raspy voice said.

Caroline smiled and stepped inside the house. Annie looked up when she entered the kitchen. She was mixing batter in a large bowl. The wood stove had been lit and the heat filled the room. The window facing the garden had been opened and the lace curtains were billowing in a light breeze. As before, Caroline smelled a hint of cinnamon.

"Well, howdy, Caroline. Ain't you a sight for these old eyes?"

"Hi, Annie, I hope you don't mind me dropping by," Caroline replied, removing her jacket and gloves, placing them on the table. "I'm sorry it took me so long to come back for a visit."

Hannah covered her mouth with her hands and giggled. "Caroline said she missed me, Granny, so she come right back to see me."

Granny smiled at Hannah and handed her the wooden spoon which was covered in cake batter, and then she turned and looked at Caroline. "Nonsense, child," she said, as she poured the batter into a cake pan. "You're always welcome here anytime. How you been faring?"

"I'm fine, Annie. And you and Hannah?"

"As you can see, we're as right as rain."

"Granny's making an apple upside down cake," Hannah said to Caroline as she licked the spoon. A good portion of the batter was on her face, nose and some of it had somehow made it to her hair.

"That sounds delicious," Caroline said, smacking her lips.

"What's your favourite cake in the whole world?" Hannah asked, licking her fingers and then wiping her mouth with the back of her hand.

"Oh, I like banana cream pie."

"What's that?" Hannah asked a puzzled look on her face.

Caroline quietly scolded herself for answering so carelessly. Not a lot of people could afford bananas and probably it was impossible for Annie to get any living this far away from town.

"It's something new."

"You'll have to give Granny the recipe the next time you come."

"Of course, I will."

"Why don't you girls sit down and enjoy a glass of buttermilk and some sugar cookies," Annie said as she put the cake pan inside the oven. "Caroline would you mind pouring some into those two mugs? The buttermilk's over on the counter."

Caroline did as she was bid and sat down next to Hannah. When they had finished, Caroline took the mugs and rinsed them in the tepid water lying in the dish basin. She dried them with a burlap towel and then placed them in the cupboard.

"Can Caroline stay for supper, Granny?" Hannah asked.

"I'm sorry, but I can't stay very long," Caroline

replied. "I have to get back and finish my chores."

"Land sakes, child, there'll be plenty of time for you to visit and get home afore your granddaddy gets back."

Caroline stared at Annie in astonishment. How could Annie know that Grandpa wasn't home?

"I would love to stay, but it'll take me over an hour just to get down the mountain, and I have to get supper started. Grandpa hates eating late."

"Sounds like that Grandpa of your'n is a might testy. Don' he allow you any time off for play, child?"

"There's not much time for play, there's so much that needs to be done around the house. Besides, I'm much too old to be playing."

"They's your Grandpa's words, not your'n."

Caroline stared uncomfortably at the floor, not sure how to respond.

"Don' you fret now, child. It's your choice and I'll respect your decision."

For a few seconds, there was silence in the kitchen. Suddenly, Annie walked over to the window, her back turned away from Caroline. "Afore you go, there's one thing I'd like you to do."

"Yes, ma'am."

"I want you to meet Alice and Eva."

"Who are Alice and Eva?" Caroline enquired.

"They're Hannah's dolls, but they're real special."

For a moment, Caroline thought Annie was teasing. Surely, she did not think a fifteen year old girl was interested in dolls? Sometimes old people said things that left her completely baffled.

Hannah hopped down from the kitchen chair and ran over to Caroline. Taking her hand, she pulled her towards the back door.

"Come on, Caroline, they're outside in the garden."

Caroline shrugged and followed Hannah outside.

They headed towards the lilacs bushes. A free-standing trellis was located next to a huge cottonwood tree and underneath was a small table and two chairs.

Hannah excitedly pulled Caroline over to the table and pushed her down onto the closest chair. Caroline awkwardly perched on the edge hoping she would not fall off or break it.

On top of the table was a miniature glass tea set and next to the table was a cradle holding two dolls wrapped in a home-made quilt.

Hannah grabbed one of the dolls and handed it to Caroline. "This is Eva and that's her sister Alice. They're my best friends in the whole world."

"Hannah, they're beautiful," Caroline replied, as she held the doll in her arms.

Caroline sat for a short while, watching Hannah play. She thought of how lonely it must be for the little girl, living so far away from other families, and not having any playmates. It brought back memories of her own childhood, although she had always preferred riding and exploring in the woods. Playing with her dolls was for the long winter nights when it was too cold to go outside.

"Are the men working in the barn?" Caroline enquired, as it seemed very quiet and she had not noticed any movement in the yard.

"No, 'member I told you. They're away and me and Granny are taking care of everything all by ourselves."

Caroline nodded and assumed that Hannah's father and the boys had again picked up work in the valley. Being away from each other so often during the year must have been hard on the family, especially Anna and Hannah. It had to be lonely for both of them.

Caroline played with Hannah for a while. They sipped make-believe tea in the little cups and ate make-believe cake. Hannah had an active imagination and Caroline found she was enjoying herself. All too soon, she realized it was time to leave.

After she had returned to the kitchen to retrieve her jacket and gloves, she thanked Annie. Then she strolled to the front, untied Ebony and climbed into the saddle. Suddenly Hannah came running around the side of the house, carrying a large bouquet of lilacs. "Caroline, I brought you some lilacs."

The young girl walked towards Ebony, but Annie overtook her and placed her hand on her arm, shaking her head. Noticing the puzzled look on Caroline's face, she quickly dropped her hand. Taking the bouquet, she handed it to Caroline.

"Since Hannah went to all that trouble picking them, don't see why you shouldn't take them with you."

Caroline reached over and took the cluster of flowers, confused at Annie's sudden change in her decision. Hannah had wrapped a piece of burlap around the stems.

"Thank you, Hannah, you're very thoughtful."

Hannah went and sat on the steps. Annie placed her right hand on Caroline's leg and then looked up at her.

"You make sure you come back soon. There's still a lot to be done."

Caroline nodded, wondering what Annie had meant. She supposed everyone got a bit peculiar as they got older, but for some reason she did not believe that was the case with Annie. The old woman was the most stable person she had ever met, and Caroline sensed she never said anything unless she meant it.

Caroline trotted Ebony down the roadway and then headed across the field towards the trail. True to form, the horse fidgeted until he passed the mountain ash and then almost immediately settled down.

She walked Ebony cautiously down the mountain path, as there were still skiffs of snow lying on the trail. She suddenly remembered she had not asked Annie about the weather being so different, but for some reason it did not seem that important, so she shrugged the thought aside.

When they got to level ground she had Ebony pick up his pace, and when they arrived at the roadway, she galloped over to the barn. She was surprised to see that Pete was still in the corral working with the horses. She felt a twinge of guilt in leaving him alone with the chores and she hastily apologized. "I'm sorry I'm so late, Pete. I'll get supper started right away. Has Grandpa been back long?"

"I'd prefer lunch before you make supper. You've only been gone a couple of hours. And you know your grandpa won't be back until later this afternoon."

Caroline's heart started beating rapidly. She said nothing to Pete. She took Ebony into the barn and placed him in his stall, her thoughts in turmoil. What was happening to her? This was the second time she had lost complete track of time.

Reaching into the saddle bag, she took out the lilacs. At first she wasn't exactly sure what she was holding. The flowers were dead and shrivelled and Caroline watched in amazement as the dried petals drifted slowly to the floor. The burlap blanket had yellowed, and when Caroline touched it, the material fell apart in her hands.

She grabbed the edge of the stall, taking deep breaths. There had to be an explanation for everything that was happening.

She had not been sleeping well lately, worrying that Grandpa would sell Ebony to Mr. Mitchell, and hoping he wouldn't find out about Scott. Maybe it was finally catching up on her. If only she had someone to talk to about her worries.

Chapter 7
The Terrible Twosome and Hurtful Words

Rather than stay in the lunchroom during the noon break, Caroline and Suzanne often went to the Chalmers' house, as it was only a few blocks away from the school. Scott and Wesley usually joined them, unless they had baseball or basketball practice.

Caroline always packed her own lunch, because she did not want to impose on Mrs. Chalmers as she knew it was expensive feeding a large family. She also noticed Mrs. Chalmers was expecting another baby, but she did not say anything to Suzanne about it, as she knew it wasn't polite to talk about such things.

It was a warm, balmy Wednesday, and the four friends were eating outside in the back yard, sitting at a small card table Mrs. Chalmers had set up for them. Even though they lived in the middle of town, the Chalmers had almost two acres of land. There was a fenced paddock and a horse shelter at the far end of the lot where Scott's bay gelding, Monty and an older horse called Colby were pastured.

Closer to the house was a chicken coop and a large garden, which helped to feed the large growing family.

"You're coming to the rodeo next week, aren't you Caroline?" Scott asked. He was competing in the calf roping this year.

"I don't know. Pete will probably go as he likes to visit with his friends."

"Are you going to ask your Grandpa if you can go?" Suzanne asked, taking a bite of her apple and staring candidly into Caroline's eyes.

"I suppose so," Caroline replied sullenly, realizing her friend was pushing her for an answer.

"Look, my dad is the head announcer at the rodeo,"

Wesley said. "Maybe if I ask he'll talk to your Grandpa."

"I don't know, Wesley," Caroline said uncomfortably. "That's probably not a good idea."

"For heaven sakes, why not?" Suzanne asked angrily.

"Suzanne, I've gone over this a hundred times with you. I'd just as soon not get Grandpa worked up."

"You know, Caroline you have to start standing up for yourself one of these days," Scott said, interrupting her. "Who knows? Maybe one of these times he'll say yes."

Caroline stared at Scott in shock. He was always so supportive of her, yet this time she sensed frustration in his voice.

Her face flushed in embarrassment. How could she possibly make him understand? She was terrified of provoking Grandpa and making him angry enough he'd take Mr. Mitchell up on his offer to buy Ebony. For some reason, Caroline felt that if she stayed on Grandpa's good side, he would let her keep Ebony a while longer. She did not want to discuss it, especially when Wesley was around, because he might bring the matter up with his father, who in turn would start pressuring Grandpa for an answer.

Everyone finished eating their lunch in silence. Mrs. Chalmers came outside and reminded them how late it was getting. Suzanne and Wesley walked ahead of them, chatting companionably, while Caroline followed with Scott. She was quiet and refused to look at him; his sharp words had hurt her.

Suddenly, the Terrible Twosome came tearing out from behind a huge poplar tree. Charlie had a Davey Crockett hat perched on the top of his head, and Teddy was wearing a gun and holster around his waist, with a red Roy Rogers cowboy hat hanging by a string down his back.

"Caroline and Scott sitting under a tree. K-i-s-s-i-n-g. First comes love, then..." they sang boisterously, making so much noise they were probably heard blocks away.

Scott let out a wild whoop and chased the giggling boys. He grabbed one under each arm, spinning them around until they were dizzy. The twins squealed in delight and Scott told them if they didn't stop pestering them, he would throw their hats into the top branches of the tree. He placed the two boys on the ground and they quickly disappeared down the sidewalk.

"Look, I'm sorry if I made you mad," Scott said quietly, when he returned to where Caroline was standing. "I just wish your Grandpa would let you come to town sometimes on the weekends, so that we can go out. What harm can that do?"

"You know how he feels about me dating. And the only way I can get into town is if he drives, and he only does that when there's a meeting with the other ranchers or to pick up supplies."

"So, ask him if you can come along, tell him you want to visit with Suzanne."

"Scott, I can't lie to him."

"You're right, I'm sorry. But promise me you'll keep on trying, okay? Suzanne, Wesley and I hang out at the soda shop, and its tons of fun."

Scott took her hand and they walked quietly down the sidewalk. When the school came into sight, Caroline pulled her hand away. She did not want anyone to see them because they weren't going steady, and she did not want to get a bad reputation. Sundre was a small town and it wouldn't take long for word to get back to Grandpa.

For the rest of the afternoon, Caroline mulled over what Scott had said. She had finally decided to bring the matter up with Grandpa, maybe he would be willing to listen to her if he knew they were only going to the soda shop to talk.

After arriving home from school, instead of cutting through the woods, she headed across the yard and walked towards the tool shed where she spotted Grandpa tinkering with his tractor. He had grease smeared up his arms and across his forehead and was muttering under his breath. Caroline knew he was worried, as a new tractor was not something they could afford to buy.

She walked slowly past the shed, stopped and turned around. Grandpa lifted his head and she waved. Suddenly, her courage dissolved and saying nothing, she continued to the back of the house and into the kitchen. Pete was sitting at the table, drinking a cup of coffee and eating a piece of the carrot loaf she had baked on the weekend.

"Well, you're home early. No shortcuts through the woods today?"

She smiled at him, cut a piece of the loaf and poured a glass of milk.

"Uncle Pete," she said, as she sat down. "Are you going to the rodeo this weekend?"

"You bet, wouldn't miss it for the world."

"Do you think you can talk Grandpa into letting me go?'

"Why the sudden interest?"

"I've always liked the rodeo, you know that."

"Wouldn't be because one of the contestants is a certain dark haired boy called Scott, now would it?"

Caroline's face turned red. She wondered how Pete knew what was going on when she hadn't mentioned anything to him. Before she could answer, he reached over and placed his hand over hers and chuckled quietly.

"Don't see as how it would hurt to talk to your Grandpa, heck there was a time when he never missed a rodeo."

"Really?"

"Yup, if I recollect right, he even competed a couple of times. I believe it was sheep riding."

"Sheep riding!" Caroline exclaimed, trying hard to not laugh out loud.

"Course, he was about seven years old at the time."

"Oh, Uncle Pete, stop joking around," Caroline chuckled.

Caroline finished her snack, and quickly jumped up. "I better start supper, I have lots of homework tonight."

Lying in bed that night, she angrily pounded her pillow, annoyed she had lost her nerve and had not talked to Grandpa as planned. Scott would be disappointed and she knew he had every right to be. Why did she find it so hard to talk to Grandpa?

Her mind shifted to Pete and she wondered if he had had a chance to talk to Grandpa yet about the rodeo. There was no sense in worrying about it, because no matter how much she pestered him, Pete never did anything in a hurry. She would just have to wait until morning.

Chapter 8

Calf Roping Competition and Ferris Wheel Ride

Caroline was packing her lunch for school when Pete and Grandpa walked into the kitchen. Grandpa poured himself a cup of coffee and sat down at the table. He took a couple of swallows and then he turned and looked at Caroline. She nervously picked at a loose thread on her sweater.

"Pete tells me you want to go to the rodeo this weekend?"

Caroline nodded.

"I wasn't going to go since spring round-up starts in a couple of days and there's lots of work to be done around here, but as Pete pointed out, we're short a couple of hands, and since every cowboy in Alberta will be there, it's probably a good idea to go."

"You mean I can go?"

"As long as you have all your chores done on time."

"I will, I promise."

Caroline could hardly wait to get to school. She made a beeline to Suzanne's locker and found Scott and Wesley there as well. When Scott found out she would be coming, he grabbed her hand and gave it a squeeze. Caroline hastily pulled back, giving him a warning look.

Saturday arrived and the sun shone through Caroline's bedroom window, spreading its warmth throughout the room. She was up and dressed and had Ebony's stall cleaned in record time. Then she raced back to the kitchen, fried bacon and scrambled some eggs. Grandpa and Pete seemed to take forever to finish eating, but soon they were in the truck heading towards town.

The rodeo grounds were just west of Sundre and the parking lot was almost full by the time they arrived. Grandpa parked the old Ford pickup under a huge poplar.

Before they got out of the cab, he reached inside his jacket pocket and pulled out two one dollar bills. “Here,” he said to Caroline. “That should cover the gate cost and a little extra in case you get hungry.”

“It’s okay Grandpa, I only need one dollar, I don’t have to get anything to eat,” Caroline replied, returning one of the dollar bills to him.

Grandpa frowned, shook his head and then pushed the money back into her hands.

“Two dollars isn’t going to break us,” he said sharply.

“Yes, sir,” Caroline answered, as she quickly put the money in her jacket pocket.

Suzanne and Wesley were waiting by the main entrance. Scott was nowhere in sight and she assumed he was with Monty in the exercise field behind the arena.

They found a place in the third row in the middle of the bleachers. The view would be spectacular. The sun was hot for May, so Caroline pulled her hat brim down to cover her face.

She glanced around the stadium; the spectators were talking or greeting friends who joined them in the stand. The galloping horses in the arena caused swirls of dust to dissipate into the air.

Soon the stands were full and the microphone squealed annoyingly. The crowds quieted as Mr. Mitchell introduced himself and the rest of the judges.

His loud voice reverberated throughout the stadium. Wesley laughed and pointed at the judge’s box. “Dad fractures me.”

Suzanne and Caroline laughed along with him. Mr. Mitchell had a deep resonating voice, but over the loudspeaker, it sounded distant and tinny.

“When does the calf roping event start?” Caroline asked.

“It’s after the wild horse race and the barrel racing,”

Suzanne answered.

Caroline thought the wild horse race was a hoot. Each team was comprised of two riders and their objective was to rope one of the horses, get a saddle on its back, and then race to the far end of the arena without getting bucked off. Bodies were dragged through the dirt by the uncooperative horses. Just when it looked as if the horses would come out the winners, two seasoned cowboys crossed the winning line and the crowds cheered loudly.

The next event was the barrel racing. Caroline noticed that two of the competitors were girls from her school. She knew that Ebony was faster than either of their horses and she wished she could have been competing, because the prize money was fifty dollars. Ebony needed a new saddle and she would have been able to buy one with that kind of money. Caroline knew that Grandpa would never agree to let her compete in barrel racing; the rodeo was a man's world.

The calf roping event was next. The audience cheered and yelled loudly, waiting for the first participant to appear. The runway where the calves were held was off to the right. Suddenly the chute operator pulled a lever and the door opened. Almost immediately, a rider galloped after the released calf. Caroline marvelled at the dexterity of the horse and the rider.

"That's Josh MacDiarmid," Wesley said. "They have a ranch near Red Deer. He made pretty good time."

"But Scott is better," Suzanne said faithful to her brother.

The second contestant failed to rope the calf and the bystanders moaned in sympathy for the young man. Caroline knew how disappointed he was, as he would only get one chance.

Suzanne looked down at the program, then turned and looked at Caroline. "Scott's next," she whispered.

Caroline sat on the edge of her seat, her heart

beating wildly. She saw Scott in the pen next to the calf chute, waiting for the operator to pull the lever down. Suddenly the calf tore out of the chute, heading for a straight line across the arena. Immediately Scott put Monty into a gallop. In seconds, the loop of his lariat was around the calf's neck. Monty stopped on a dime and Scott jumped off and ran to the calf. He picked it up and flipped it onto its side. He tied three of the calf's legs together with a short rope while Monty slowly backed away from the calf to keep the tension steady. Then Scott threw his hands in the air to stop the clock.

He mounted Monty and moved him forward to relax the tautness of the rope. Monty and Scott worked together as if they were one. Caroline understood the bond that existed between them, as she felt the same way about Ebony.

There were three more contestants after Scott. One of the riders clocked a faster time, but received a 10-second penalty because he mistimed his cue and his horse broke the barrier before it was released.

Then the calf-roping competition was over. The microphone squealed loudly and Mr. Mitchell announced the winner.

"The winner is Scott Chalmers from Sundre with a clocked time of 7.8 seconds. Good riding, young man."

Caroline jumped up and down and hugged Suzanne. Wesley was madly waving his cowboy hat above his head and the crowd was cheering wildly, happy that the winner was from their home town. Competition was always fierce among the small communities on the rodeo circuit.

Scott joined them in the bleachers and sat down next to Caroline. People patted him on his back and shook his hand. He grabbed Caroline's hand and she gave it a squeeze.

"Scott, you're wonderful. That was the most exciting race I've ever seen."

"Exciting enough to go out with me?"

Caroline stopped smiling and released his hand. Why did it have to end like this every time?

"Scott, please?"

"Caroline, I'm sorry. I shouldn't have said that. I was just excited about winning."

"Let's go to the fairway," Suzanne said. "There's going to be an hour intermission before the bareback riding starts."

The four friends left their seats and walked over to the fairgrounds.

"Let's go on the Ferris wheel?" Wesley suggested. "It's only five cents a ride."

Soon, they had bought their tickets and were sitting in their seats. The Ferris wheel started turning and Caroline hung on tightly to the bar. She did not want to tell Scott she had never been on the Ferris wheel before, or for that matter, on any kind of ride.

The first few times it went around Caroline kept her eyes closed. Then she opened then and saw that Scott was watching her, a grin on his face. She hadn't fooled him a bit.

"Oh, Scott, it's so beautiful up here. Look you can see the Rocky Mountains in the distance."

"Yup, and there's Eagle Mountain. Your place should be over there and Wesley's is right next to it," he said, pointing off to his right. He casually reached over and put his arm around her shoulders.

Caroline grinned and then suddenly turned serious. "Scott, can I ask you a question?"

"Sure."

"You might think it's weird?"

"Oh, good," he said jokingly. "I love weird questions."

"Have you ever felt as if things were all off kilter, you know, almost as if time was standing still?"

"Sure, I guess. Do you mean like when you sleep really hard, and when you wake up, you're kind of disoriented?"

"A little like that, but not quite. Have you ever done something, um, I'm not sure how to say it."

"Wow, this sounds pretty serious."

"Okay, let's say you go somewhere or do something and a couple of hours pass by, at least you think a couple of hours have passed, when in fact, it's really only a few minutes"

Scott stared into the distance. "Did something like that happen to you?"

"It's happened to me a couple of times. I thought I was going crazy."

"I wouldn't worry about it. Maybe you were so wrapped up in what you were doing, you lost track of time."

"I suppose so," Caroline remarked, although she knew Scott's explanation was not plausible. She decided to drop the matter.

"Scott, you've done some riding on Eagle Mountain and I know you're interested in the history of that area. Have you ever come across any farms?"

"There used to be some homesteads higher up, but that was years ago. It was almost impossible to make a living. Over time, most of the farms were abandoned, and those who stayed were bought out by the Government. The land was eventually designated as Crown land and then opened to free range grazing. Some of the homesteaders bought property in the foothills, like the Mitchells and your family, for that matter. It was a good move, because the land was more fertile, and the weather less harsh, which made it perfect for ranching and growing wheat."

"The weather was less harsh?"

"Sure, only makes sense. The higher up you lived, the shorter the growing season."

"I guess so."

"Why do you ask?"

"No reason, just curious."

They did not talk for a while, but continued to enjoy the ride. Caroline scanned the fairgrounds, excited about being so high above the crowds. Suddenly she froze. Grandpa and Pete were standing next to the admission booth and Grandpa was staring right at her.

By the time the ride was over, Caroline was a nervous wreck. There was no use in pretending she hadn't seen Grandpa watching her. She walked over to where he and Pete were standing and waited until Suzanne and Wesley had joined them.

"This is Scott and Suzanne Chalmers," Caroline said, as she faced Grandpa. "And you know Wesley."

"How do you do, Mr. Lindstrom?" Scott said, reaching over and shaking Grandpa's hand.

"And this is Pete Morgan," Caroline continued, introducing him to her friends.

Pete smiled and shook everyone's hand. When he got to Scott he said. "Congratulations, young man. That was some of the nicest calf roping I've seen in a long time."

"Thank you, sir," Scott said. "I understand you've done some competing yourself?"

"Yep, when I was young and foolish."

Everyone laughed and Wesley jabbed Scott with his elbow.

"The next events are about to start," Grandpa said. "You kids planning on watching?"

The four friends all nodded their heads in unison.

"I thought as much. Pete and I are going to join Mr. Mitchell for a while. When it's over, meet us at the exit, Caroline."

The rest of the afternoon sped by far too quickly. After the bareback riding, there was the bull riding, which, according to Caroline, was the most spectacular event of the day. She hoped that Scott would never want to compete in it because it was dangerous and there were a lot of injuries and even deaths. When Caroline mentioned her concerns to him, he just laughed and said. "I've got a couple of years to wait. Dad won't let me ride until after I turn eighteen."

"And Mom said over her dead body," Suzanne said, overhearing Caroline and Scott's conversation.

All too soon, it was time to leave. When they got to the bottom of the bleachers, Mr. Mitchell waved Wesley over and told him they had to leave right away, as he had some errands to do in town before they went home. Caroline found it hard to look directly at the rancher. She knew his interest in Ebony was purely business, but she still resented his offer.

Caroline, Suzanne and Scott walked over to the exit. Grandpa and Pete were talking to Mr. and Mrs. Chalmers.

"Looks like the kids are here, get back to me as soon as you can, Grant," Grandpa said to Mr. Chalmers.

"Yes, sir, I will."

Caroline looked questioningly at Scott, but he just shrugged his shoulders. She was quiet on the drive back home. Grandpa and Pete talked about the round-up and the extra hands they had hired. Her mind was wandering when she suddenly heard Scott's name come up in the conversation.

"We could use him and his horse," Grandpa said.

"Grant said he'd talk to Scott tonight. I'm sure he'll call you sometime today, probably after supper," Pete replied.

"Sure was a smart decision I made having that telephone put in," Grandpa said, as he shifted gears in the old truck.

Caroline swung her head around and looked at Pete, her mouth gaping open. Pete winked at her and then he turned and looked out the passenger window.

Chapter 9
Cigarettes and Red Lipstick

Supper was finished, and the dishes washed and put away when the telephone rang. Caroline had been waiting for the call and she raced over and quickly picked up the receiver.

"Hello," she said, slightly out of breath.

"Hi, Caroline, it's me, Scott."

"Hi, Scott."

"Can I talk to your Grandpa?"

"He's in the living room, just a minute and I'll go get him."

"Thanks, and Caroline, I had a great time today at the rodeo."

"Thanks, I did, too."

"So, have you talked to your Grandpa yet, about letting you go out? Wesley's putting on a party next Saturday."

Suddenly, Grandpa's voice boomed from down the hall. "Is that Scott Chalmers on the phone, Caroline?"

"Yes, Grandpa," Caroline answered.

Before she had time to say anything more, Grandpa walked into the kitchen and took the receiver out of her hand.

"Hello," he shouted. For some reason, he always yelled whenever he talked on the phone. Caroline had given up trying to explain to him that it wasn't necessary and all she could hope for was that the person on the other end didn't have the receiver too close to their ear.

Grandpa nodded his head a few times and then said loudly. "I'll see you tomorrow." Without asking Caroline if she wanted to talk to Scott, he hung up.

Caroline followed him into the living room, hoping to find out more.

"That young Chalmers on the phone?" Pete asked without lifting his head from his checker game.

"Yup," Grandpa answered, as he lowered himself into his chair. "He said he'd be happy to help with the branding, and he's bringing his horse with him, too."

"Good, we're lucky he agreed to come. Most of the experienced cowhands have been picked up already and we would have been short. With Scott's help, we should get finished on time."

Before she went to sleep that night, Caroline took the broach out of her jewellery box and looked at it. She wished she could wear it tomorrow, but having Scott around all day was more exciting.

The next morning, she was up and dressed before the sun peeked over the tree tops. She put on her denim skirt and a cotton blouse, although she would have preferred wearing her jeans. With so many people around the ranch for the next few days, Grandpa would have been annoyed if she had not dressed appropriately.

The spring round-up was the largest of the year. Many of the smaller ranchers in the area participated and usually it was held at Eagle Ridge Ranch because of its proximity to Eagle Mountain. The cattle had to be sorted by owner, branded, earmarked, and returned to the grazing lands to free range until the fall. Caroline would help the women in the kitchen cooking meals and supplying fresh water and coffee to the hard working cowhands throughout the day.

Pete always rode Ebony and Grandpa preferred riding Riverboat. The big dapple needed a strong hand to keep him in line. His doggedness was invaluable in separating the calves from their mothers and keeping the herd calm.

Before she had the breakfast dishes cleared away from the table, the first pick-up drove up the driveway. Vehicles were parked all the way down the roadway from the house to the main gate. People were mingling, greeting each other and getting caught up on gossip. The kitchen was soon full of laughing women and excited children, running up and down the hallways, slamming doors and getting underfoot.

The table groaned under the weight of the food, the counter was covered with casserole dishes and the ice box and the root cellar were crammed full.

The women set up wooden horses under the huge poplar trees next to the fire pit. They laid boards across the tops and made make-shift tables, which they covered with vinyl table cloths. Then they hauled out coffee pots, mugs, spoons, sugar and fresh cream. It wasn't long before every cowhand was holding a mug of steaming coffee. At noon, the hungry men would expect a hot lunch and then a larger meal would be served later in the evening.

Suddenly, a horn beeped and Caroline looked up. She recognized the Chalmers' truck as it drove towards the house, a horse trailer hitched to the back. Suzanne was sitting in the front with her parents and Scott was balancing on the tailgate in the box of the truck.

Suzanne jumped out of the truck and Caroline stared in astonishment. Her friend was dressed in a tight-fitting black skirt, a pink long-sleeved cashmere sweater, and a matching pink ribbon holding back her long hair. She was wearing bright red lipstick and green eye shadow, which make her black hair and eyes stand out vividly. Caroline thought Suzanne looked like she was eighteen years old and was surprised Mrs. Chalmers would let her dress like that, especially at an event where so many of their neighbours were present.

Mr. Chalmers got out and walked around to the passenger door. He helped Mrs. Chalmers as she climbed awkwardly out of the cab. Caroline noticed that she had gotten larger and thought how hot and uncomfortable she looked.

Mrs. Chalmers handed Suzanne two large bowls, then turned and took out two more, handing them to Caroline.

Caroline noticed Scott watching her and she smiled back at him. He jumped down from the box. By now, Pete and a small group of cowhands had walked over from the corral and were standing at the back of the trailer, waiting for Scott to unlatch the door. Scott slowly backed Monty out, although he did not have any problem with the gentle horse. He kept looking over at Caroline to see if she was watching.

"Come along, girls," Mrs. Chalmers smiled, witnessing the exchange of glances between Caroline and Scott. "We have chores to do."

Caroline peeked under the dish towels covering the bowls. There was a roast, two chickens and a large ham.

"Oh, Mrs. Chalmers, you didn't have to prepare this much food."

"Nonsense, Caroline, I had plenty of time yesterday while you kids were at the rodeo. Believe me, I know how hungry a working man can get. Scott could pack away one of these chickens all by himself."

Caroline looked up and locked eyes with Scott. He grinned and then winked, making her blush. She could sense him watching her as she walked up the porch steps.

Mrs. Chalmers greeted the women who were gathered in the kitchen and in no time at all they were discussing babies and recipes.

Suzanne and Caroline stood at the counter, listening to everyone talking at the same time. Suzanne bent over and whispered in Caroline's ear. "I'm so glad I came, we can spend the whole day together."

"Where is the Terrible Twosome?"

"They're at home with Grandma Chalmers. They wanted to come, but Mom said this was no place for two young rambunctious boys. They would have run her ragged."

"I don't know how she does it, taking care of all you kids and then cooking all that food yesterday."

"You mean because she's going to have another baby?"

Caroline nodded, her face reddening with embarrassment.

"Isn't it just keen? I hope we have a girl. We have enough boys as it is."

Caroline laughed along with Suzanne. "You're so lucky having such a big family."

Suzanne shrugged, obviously not as impressed with the idea as Caroline.

"Mr. Mitchell wanted Scott to work for him today," she said changing the subject, "but Scott decided to come here instead."

Caroline giggled and put her index finger up to her mouth, warning her friend to keep her voice down.

"Oh, Caroline, my mom knows about you and Scott."

"What do you mean?"

"That you two like each other. Besides, she's the one who gave Scott your broach. I remember at the time, she said something really funny, that she had been holding onto it long enough and it was time it was returned to the rightful owner."

When Caroline did not answer, Suzanne put her arm around her waist and gave her a hug. "Don't worry, Mom won't say anything to anyone? She's really great about keeping secrets."

Mrs. Chalmers walked towards the counter and Suzanne and Caroline stopped talking. "Everything's under control in the kitchen, so why don't you girls run off and visit with each other. It's so noisy in here you can't hear yourself think."

They thanked Mrs. Chalmers and quickly left.

"Come on, let's go watch the branding for a while," Suzanne suggested. Caroline was surprised that Suzanne wanted to go down to the corrals, as she usually avoided outdoor activities with a vengeance.

They were half way across the yard, when Suzanne stopped and reached inside her pocket. She took out a pack of cigarettes and a lighter. Caroline watched in amazement as she lit the cigarette and inhaled deeply.

"When did you start smoking?" she asked.

"A little while ago, you want one?"

"No, thanks."

"I suppose your Grandpa doesn't believe in girls smoking? "

"No, not really," Caroline said, "and I don't either, they're so smelly."

"Jeez, Caroline, don't wig out on me, okay?"

Caroline found it hard to believe this was the same Suzanne she had spent the day with at the rodeo just a day ago, she was behaving like an entirely different person.

"Come on," Suzanne said. "Let's go check out those cute cowboys."

The two girls arrived at the corral and Caroline noticed a couple of the young cowhands staring at Suzanne. Her friend flipped her ponytail and took a deep puff on her cigarette. For some reason, her actions embarrassed Caroline.

Without warning, Caroline thought of Annie and how disapproving the older woman would have been if she could have witnessed their behaviour. Caroline shook her head irritably. Why in the world was she thinking of Annie? It had been ages since she had seen her.

Caroline spotted Pete at the lit fire pit located at the far end of the corral. He threw in a couple of logs then turned the coals, checking to make sure it was hot enough to begin branding. He got up on Ebony and rode half way down the corral and stood next to the fence. After a calf was branded, it was Ebony's job to direct it back to the chute, bawling for its mother.

Scott and Monty were waiting by the gate of the cattle pen. As the calves were released, he or one of the ranch hands would have it roped, thrown and restrained in record time. One of the bystanders was timing the roping and in no time, a competition was soon in full swing.

Caroline looked away each time a calf was branded. She knew it was necessary and part of running a ranch, but she always felt sorry for the young animal.

Not more than ten minutes had passed when Suzanne poked Caroline's arm. "Come on, this is boring. Let's go to your room. My new clothes are getting dirty and I can feel grit in my teeth. I hate that feeling."

Caroline couldn't believe her ears. Surely, Suzanne must have known that a round-up was the last place to wear a black skirt and a cashmere sweater.

Caroline reluctantly agreed to leave, although she would have preferred to stay and watch.

When they got to her room, the two girls sat down on the bed. Suzanne took a tube of lipstick out of her pocket and handed it to Caroline. "Here," she said. "Put some on, you're always so pale."

Caroline shook her head. "I better not."

"Don't tell me you can't wear makeup either."

Not wanting Suzanne to think she was punking out, Caroline grabbed the lipstick and hurriedly put some on. She could not see what she looked like, but for some reason it made her feel uncomfortable. All she could think about was Annie's reaction and she angrily wondered why the older woman was stuck in her mind.

"Let me put your hair up," Suzanne offered. "You would look so cool if you got rid of those juvenile pigtails."

"No, I'd rather not. It's easier when I'm working around the house and the barn."

"Honestly, Caroline, if you want Scott to notice you

more, then you has to stop being such a wet rag."

"I am not a wet rag, Suzanne," Caroline said sharply. "At least I don't wear cashmere sweaters to a round-up."

"Well, at least I don't dress like a boy all the time."

The two girls stared at each other in silence and then suddenly they both started laughing. They laughed so hard the tears were flowing down their cheeks. Suddenly, a glass of water sitting on the night table flew through the air, shattering as it hit the floor. Caroline wiped her face with her sleeve and then jumped off the bed and started picking up the glass. All at once, she was overwhelmed by an overpowering aroma of lilacs. She gasped, and sat heavily on the edge of the bed.

"Caroline, are you okay?" Suzanne asked, reaching over and grabbing Caroline's arm. "You're as white as a sheet."

"Can't you smell it?" Caroline said, pointing to the floor.

"Smell what? For heaven sakes, it's only water."

"Can't you smell the lilacs?"

"I think you were in the sun too long. After we clean up this mess, let's go downstairs and sit on the porch," Suzanne suggested. Caroline heard the concern in her voice and decided to change the subject.

"That sounds like a great idea. It's so hot up here anyways."

Soon, the two girls were outside, sitting side by side on the wicker lounge. Suzanne lit another cigarette and blew the smoke casually into the air.

"Oh, there you two are," Mrs. Chalmers said as she walked around the corner. "Take these dishes and cutlery out to the tables. Lunch is almost ready."

When the two girls turned and faced Mrs. Chalmers, she scowled, giving them a disapproving look, but said nothing. Caroline quickly grabbed the utensils and raced over to the tables. She rubbed her hand across her mouth, trying to wipe off the red lipstick.

A metal basin, soap and towels were placed on a tree trunk and the cowhands lined up to wash their hands and faces. Caroline kept an eye on the water, making sure it was replaced when it got too dirty.

Scott was laughing and joking with the men sitting on either side of him. Periodically he would lift his head and smile at Caroline while she brought trays of food to the table or poured coffee into the mugs. Caroline pretended to not notice him and kept her head down. She sensed Grandpa watching her from the far end of the table. If he should say anything about the lipstick, or make a scene, she would die of embarrassment.

After the men had eaten and returned to the corral, the women hauled everything back into the house. They ate a quick lunch, then washed the tall stack of dishes and set everything aside for supper.

The kitchen was stifling, and soon everyone was on the porch, or lounging on blankets spread out on the lawn under the huge poplars and cottonwoods. Pitchers of lemonade were passed around and Caroline thought it was not half as good as Annie's. The women who weren't keeping the younger children occupied were knitting or mending clothes they have brought with them.

The rest of the day passed slowly. Caroline dreaded starting the wood stove, as the kitchen was already unbearable from the heat. However, there was no way of getting out of it, as the hard-working men were expecting a hot meal.

Finally, the branding was over for the day. By the time supper was finished, it was starting to get dark and comfortably cooler. A fire was started in the fire pit.

The kitchen was soon cleaned and the exhausted women went and joined the men around the campfire. Mr. Chalmers offered his seat to Mrs. Chalmers, who thanked him and sat down. Caroline watched as she massaged her lower back, her weariness etched on her face.

Two young cowboys offered their seats to Suzanne and Caroline. It wasn't until Caroline had sat down that she realized she was sitting next to Scott.

He smiled and raised his eyebrows, pointing to her lips. Suzanne giggled and Caroline gave her a disparaging look.

"I appreciate you coming out today to help, young man," Grandpa said as he walked over to Scott.

"You're welcome, sir," Scott replied, reaching over his shoulder and shaking Grandpa's hand.

"I could use you tomorrow and the next day, if you're available."

"I'd love to come, but I don't think Mom and Dad will let me miss school."

"We know you like nothing better than riding Monty and doing ranch work," Mr. Chalmers said overhearing the conversation. "But school comes first."

Caroline would not be attending school on Monday or Tuesday as it was not unusual for students who lived on ranches or farms to be absent during spring round-up.

"You plan on ranching when you get older, Scott?" Pete asked, as he pulled a pack of cigarettes out of his shirt pocket.

"I'd sure like to, but I know how expensive it is to get started. I'm hoping to win some competitions on the rodeo circuit and maybe make enough to put down on a piece of land somewhere."

"Rodeo's a tough life. You have to win it all before you get any of the big purses, assuming you don't get injured first."

'Yes, sir, I know. That's why I plan on attending the Agricultural College in Olds after I graduate."

The cowhands listening to the conversation nodded their heads knowingly. A lot of them had participated in rodeo events, but not many of them made enough to do it full time. It was too unpredictable and was no life if you had a family. Young, unmarried cowboys could do well, if they didn't mind living in a trailer and following the circuits from town to town. The more ambitious ones aimed for the Calgary Stampede where the winnings were larger.

"That's a wise decision," Pete said. "Ranching isn't like it used to be. Everything is so mechanized now and you need to know the financial end of things as well. Also, a smart rancher needs to know the benefits of grazing leases and stock-watering reserves."

Caroline had been listening in fascination to the conversation. Hearing Scott talk about his future plans made her wonder if she wanted to marry a rancher when she got older. For that matter, she did not know if she wanted to get married at all.

One of the cowhands brought out his guitar and another produced a harmonica. Everyone was exhausted, so they quietly listened to the mournful music. Several of the younger children were sleeping in their mother's laps.

Caroline looked up at the stars and a light breeze cooled her face. She watched Mrs. Chalmers laughing and joking with Mr. Chalmers. Maybe having children didn't mean that a woman lost her independence, but she could have both and still be happy.

One thing Caroline was positive about, if she did marry a rancher, she would insist on wearing jeans and shirts whenever she wanted to. Some things were just not negotiable.

Chapter 10
A Cowboy and a Floozy

It was an early night for everyone and soon all of the vehicles were gone except for the Chalmers' truck. Most of the cowhands and their families would return in the next two days, and when the branding was finished, the cattle would be returned to the grazing lands on Eagle Mountain until fall.

Caroline and Suzanne carried the empty pots and casserole dishes to the truck, chatting happily about the events of the day. Scott was loading Monty into the back of the trailer. When he saw the two girls talking, he bolted the door and strolled over and joined them.

"I'll see you in school on Wednesday," he said to Caroline. "That should give you time to talk to your Grandpa about Wesley's party."

Caroline nodded and waited until the truck reached the gate, its headlights lighting up the trees along the roadway. She decided to check the kitchen one last time to make sure it was ready for tomorrow.

Grandpa was sitting at the table drinking a cup of coffee. He looked up when Caroline entered the room.

"What did Scott want you to talk to me about?"

Caroline stopped in her tracks. He must have overheard them talking. She sat down at the table, cleared her throat and said. "Scott was wondering if it would be alright if I went with him to a party at Wesley's house next week."

"What do you mean went with him?"

"You know, go on a date with him."

Grandpa's face turned red. Caroline knew he was angry, as she could see the vein on his forehead throbbing.

"I thought we had discussed this before, Caroline. You're far too young to be dating."

"But the party is going to be chaperoned, Mr. and Mrs. Mitchell will be home."

"Are you seeing him at school?"

"Of course, I see him at school. We're only two grades apart."

"That's not what I meant and you know it. Do you spend time alone with him?"

"Where would we spend time alone? I see him between classes and sometimes I go to the Chalmers' house for lunch. Suzanne and Wesley are there, too, and Mrs. Chalmers is always home."

"You and Scott haven't been getting serious, have you?"

Caroline stood up and walked over to the pump. She filled a glass with cold water and returned to the table and sat down, refusing to let Grandpa's comments upset her.

"You sound as if you don't trust me. I'm not stupid, Grandpa. I know how a young woman should behave in public and Scott would never do anything to jeopardize my reputation."

"That may be, but your friend Suzanne is heading straight for trouble. She dresses like a floozy, all that makeup and those tight clothes."

"Suzanne is a nice girl."

"Nice girls don't smoke or flirt openly with young cowboys. I saw the way she acted when you two were at the corral."

"She was just being friendly Grandpa."

Grandpa snorted and Caroline's face turned red with embarrassment. Suzanne only had herself to blame for acting the way she did. Grandpa wouldn't have been the only one who noticed her behaviour.

"And what's that gunk all over your face?" he asked sharply.

"It's just lipstick."

"Make sure you wash it off and I don't want to see you wearing it again. You're getting as wild as that girl."

"Fine, I'll wash it off," Caroline replied tiredly

"She's not the kind of girl I want you to be friends with."

"What do you mean?"

"Exactly what I said. I don't want you seeing her anymore."

Caroline sat in stunned silence, glaring angrily at her grandfather.

"Suzanne is my best friend."

"Maybe you better find another best friend. From now on both Suzanne and her brother are off limits."

"You didn't feel that way about Scott when he came and helped you with the branding."

"Having him work for me and you spending time with him are two entirely different matters."

"That's completely unfair. All Scott and I do is talk. Nothing has happened."

"And I'm making sure nothing will."

Caroline jumped up and her chair fell with a crash to the floor. "Well, Scott likes me and I like him. You can't stop me from seeing him at school."

"The school term is almost over, and unless you want me picking you up every day after school, you will do as I tell you."

Caroline spun around and ran towards the stairs, almost colliding with Pete who had just come in from outside. She ignored him when he asked her what was wrong. She raced up the stairs and down the hallway to her bedroom, slamming the door as hard as she could. She lay down on her bed, seething in anger. This time Grandpa had gone too far.

The next two days went agonizingly slow. Caroline stayed inside the house, helping with the meals or watching over the young children so that the mothers could take a break.

Finally, the branding was over and on Wednesday she returned to school. The moment Scott saw the look on her face he knew the news was not good. She told Scott that Grandpa would not allow her to go to the party, but she did not mention what he had said about not seeing him and Suzanne anymore. Caroline had no intention of losing Suzanne's friendship, but she secretly wished Suzanne would stop smoking and wearing so much makeup. It would not take long before some of their classmates started talking behind her back and Caroline knew that if Suzanne got a bad reputation, she would be stuck with it forever. People in small towns had long memories.

Caroline's sullenness began to affect everyone around her. Suzanne spent most of her time with Wesley. If Caroline saw Scott coming down the hallway, she would dodge into the girl's bathroom, or head down another corridor, anything to avoid talking to him. She was afraid she would break down and tell him everything. Scott would not hesitate to confront Grandpa and Caroline would just die of mortification if it ever came to that.

The end of June arrived, exams were over and school was out for the term. Caroline went to clean out her locker and was surprised to see Suzanne and Scott waiting for her.

"We couldn't let you leave without saying goodbye, no matter how much of a party pooper you've become," Suzanne said.

"Are you going to come into town during the summer?" Scott asked.

"Probably not. There's always so much work to be done around the ranch."

"What about your birthday in August?"

Caroline shrugged.

"This is ridiculous," Scott said. "I'll be visiting Wesley during the summer. Maybe we can meet somewhere."

"Call me," Caroline said. "And we'll work something out."

If she had to, she would sneak away and Grandpa would never have to know. She refused to let him dictate who she could be friends with.

When she got home, she went to her room and changed her clothes. Then she went downstairs to start preparing supper. She was surprised to see Pete sitting at the table.

"Caroline, I want to talk to you."

Caroline walked over to the ice box and took out some left over ham and potatoes for supper.

"Your grandpa told me what happened."

Caroline looked at Pete, but said nothing.

"You can't spend the rest of your life being angry at him."

"You're taking his side," she said bitterly.

Pete stood up and walked over to where she was standing next to the stove. "I'm not taking anyone's side. You know I love you and so does your grandpa."

"As long as I jump when he gives me an order or I don't talk back to him."

"Now, you know that's not true. Yes, he's a hard man and strict, but that's just his way."

"Lately, he's almost unbearable. I just don't understand why I can't see Scott and Suzanne."

"I know it hasn't been easy for you, living with two grumpy old men. Your grandpa just doesn't want anything bad to happen to you."

"He has to learn to trust me sometime. I'm almost fifteen, Pete. I can't stay buried in this old house forever."

Pete shook his head sadly. "I know, I know, but he has a lot on his mind right now. You're old enough to know we're going through some tough financial troubles and he's worried about the ranch."

"Well, maybe he wouldn't have been in this fix if he had kept this place up. It's falling down around our heads."

Caroline realized she was not being fair but she was too upset to feel any remorse about what she had just said. She turned and raced upstairs to her room, but not before she saw the distressed look on Pete's face.

Chapter 11
Running Away and an Unexpected Visit

Grandpa's mood did not improve. Every night after supper, he would go directly to the living room to read his cattle report magazines or stare sullenly out the window. Caroline had not heard a word from Scott, which only added to her misery.

The days ahead looked bleak and she found it harder and harder to get up in the mornings and go about her chores. Her nightmares had returned and often she awoke feeling as if she hadn't slept at all. She had no appetite, was losing weight, and had dark shadows under her eyes. She knew she looked terrible. Even Ebony felt her depression and shied away from her when she saddled him or entered his stall.

Pete tried a number of times to talk to them, but to no avail. Finally, in frustration, he threw his hands up in the air, telling them that he was wiping his hands of the whole affair. He showed up for meals and then hastily retreated to the bunkhouse. Rusty had taken to sleeping there as well, sensing the tension in the house.

Caroline was staring out the kitchen window a few days later when she finally made her decision. The idea had been germinating for some time. She would go to Annie's house and ask if she could work for her room and board until she sorted out what to do with her life.

After supper, she went to her room and quietly closed her door. She took her backpack out of her closet, filled it with clothes, her hairbrush, and her personal toiletries. At the last second, she remembered the silver broach. Then she shoved her pack under her bed and waited for dark.

It wasn't long before she heard Grandpa's footsteps on the stairs and his bedroom door closing. Pete usually went to bed around the same time. She waited until she heard the back door closing downstairs and then she ran to the window and looked outside. She spotted Pete and Rusty as they walked across the yard, heading towards the bunkhouse.

She waited until her clock said 10:30 to retrieve her pack. She crept down the stairs, avoiding the steps that creaked. There was a full moon and it shone through the kitchen window. She cut two slices of bread and a chunk of ham and wrapped them in a clean dishtowel. Next, she filled her canteen with cold water. She stuffed everything in her backpack, and as a second thought, threw in an apple and some oatmeal cookies.

Caroline walked towards the root cellar. When she got to the bottom of the stairs, she grabbed a flashlight that was kept on a shelf next to the door. A rustling sound filled the room and she spun quickly. A soft glow shone in the far corner and she flicked on the flashlight. The hairs on her arms and the back of her neck stood straight up. As quickly as it had started, the noise stopped and the light disappeared.

Caroline exhaled and shook her head in frustration. How did she expect to ride all the way up Eagle Mountain alone in the dead of night, if a few noises in the root cellar spooked her?

She quickly raced up the steps, closing the heavy door behind her. Soon she was standing outside on the porch. She made out the bulky outline of the old barn on the far side of the yard. The only sounds were the chirping of crickets and a hooting owl in a nearby tree.

She hid in the overgrown thicket that bordered the yard, keeping low and hiding in the shadows. She hoped Rusty wouldn't start barking, but the old dog's hearing was not as sharp as it used to be, and thankfully the bunkhouse was on the far side of the yard.

When she arrived at the barn, she sped around to the

back and entered through the back door. Ebony greeted her with a snort and Caroline patted his neck. She felt her way over to the tack room and gathered what she needed.

She slipped the bridle over Ebony's ears and inserted the bit between his teeth. Then she threw a blanket over his back and heaved the saddle on top cinching it tightly. Caroline had done this so often, she did not need a light to see what she was doing.

She walked on the grass bordering the road, muffling the sound of Ebony's hooves. They arrived at the gate where she turned left, eventually arriving at the trail heading towards Eagle Mountain.

When the dark silhouette of the farmhouse was no longer visible, she mounted Ebony and steered him down the path. She dug the flashlight out of her pack and turned it on, pointing its beam towards the ground. There were roots and sharp rocks crossing the trail. She did not want to chance Ebony taking a fall.

She spun around nervously when she heard a muffled noise in the woods. Spanning the flashlight in a wide sweep, she peered at the closely packed trees. She spotted a pinecone lying on the mossy forest floor. Laughing nervously, she chastised herself for being so skittish.

The trail gradually became steeper. She spotted the ghostly outline of a grove of white birch, remembering she had passed them in April. She relaxed, relieved that she had not wandered off the main trail. Getting lost on the mountain in the middle of the night could be dangerous. She was not worried about running into a bear, as they usually did not bother a grown horse. The only thing that might prove to be dangerous was a cougar, but there had not been any sightings in the area for a while. The ranchers kept a close lookout for them, because it was not unforeseen for the big cat to take a calf.

When she arrived at the split in the trail, she turned

right without hesitation. The night was warm and Caroline drank most of the water from her canteen.

It wasn't long before she recognized the shape of the mountain ash, so she steered Ebony towards it. As had happened before, her arms and legs began to tingle. She could feel the warmth of her locket inside her shirt. She did not know what caused these sensations, but as they disappeared as quickly as they started, she did not let it concern her. Again, Ebony started to act up and he balked when she prodded him with her heels. She firmly ordered him to obey and he reluctantly trotted into the field.

Caroline looked around the yard in dismay. The house was dark. It struck her that Annie and Hannah were probably in bed. A person did not ride up to someone's house at this late hour and expect a friendly welcome. She had been in such a hurry to get away, she had not thought about the hour she would be arriving.

The only solution was to wait until daybreak before announcing her presence. She trotted across the field towards the roadway and headed towards the barn. When she got to the corral, she dismounted and tied Ebony to the gate. She stretched her back and stiff muscles and then she opened the heavy barn door. The smell of fresh hay and animal droppings reminded her of home.

She swept the flashlight around the barn spotting a doe-eyed Guernsey in the pen closest to the door. The other stalls were empty and she wondered if the men were away working in the valley again. She returned to the corral and untied Ebony, leading him inside. Removing his saddle, she laid it on top of a bale of hay, along with the horse blanket and her backpack. Then she led Ebony into one of the stalls and latched the door.

Grabbing the blanket and her pack, she walked over to the ladder and climbed up to the hayloft. The night had turned chilly. She stacked the hay into a pile making a make-shift bed, then lay down and wrapped herself tightly in the horse blanket. The straw was a bit prickly, but she was wearing her jeans and denim jacket and was not uncomfortable.

She placed her backpack under her head as a pillow. Once she was comfortably settled, she remembered to shut off the flashlight to preserve the battery.

There was a window high above her and she could see the stars twinkling in the sky. A brook flowed nearby.

She sighed deeply, rolled over, closed her eyes and was soon fast asleep.

Chapter 12
A Guernsey Cow and a Confusing Talk

Caroline was awaked by a rustling sound close to her head. A little head peeked out from under the straw and she stared into the eyes of a tiny mouse. It was not frightened of her, so it continued scrounging in the hay. She ran her fingers through her dishevelled hair. Opening her backpack, she found her hairbrush and combed out the snarls. Then she braided her hair, letting it fall down her back.

She was famished, and soon everything she had packed was gone. She opened her canteen and remembered she had drunk all the water. She climbed down from the loft, walked out of the barn around to the back, and over to the small creek she had heard the night before. Scooping water into her cupped hands she drank thirstily, it tasted cool and refreshing. The bright purple petals of a cluster of violets added colour to the foliage growing next to the stream.

Returning to the barn, she went and checked Ebony. He greeted her with a snort and she patted him affectionately on his neck. She found a pitchfork leaning against the wall and tossed some hay into his stall. She spotted a wooden bucket and went to the brook to fill it. Returning to the barn, she poured the water into the trough. Ebony blew on her face, then lowered his head and began eating the hay.

She left the barn and wandered towards the house. She walked around to the back and knocked on the door. It swung open and, as before, it was Hannah who greeted her.

"Boy, Caroline, you sure must like it here." she said pleasantly.

"That's because it's the nicest place in the world. Is your Granny around?"

"Yes," Hannah giggled. "She's coming right out cause she has to milk Blossom."

Then Hannah ran outside and raced around the corner of the house.

Suddenly, Annie appeared in the doorway, carrying a metal pail. She did not seem surprised to see Caroline.

"Morning, Caroline."

"Hello, Annie. When you have a few minutes, I'm wondering if I could talk to you about something."

"I'm just wandering to the barn, whyn't you join me?"

Caroline followed Annie over to the stall where the Guernsey was located. Annie placed the pail on the floor beneath the placid cow.

Hannah called from the back of the barn. "Granny, Caroline's horse is in Buck's stall."

"That's fine, your brother ain't here, so Buck don't need his stall right now. You be careful, 'cause that fidgety horse don't know you."

"Ebony's pretty level-headed. Just don't startle him from behind."

"Hannah, feed him some oats, and mind what Caroline just tol' you."

"Yes, Granny."

"Why don't you let me milk Blossom?" Caroline offered.

"That would be just dandy," Annie said, lowering herself into an old chair sitting across from the stall, which was obviously used often by the old woman. "Blossom is real gentle and don't mind strangers atall."

Caroline nodded, but not before she noticed how slow Annie's movements were. Pulling the stool over towards the cow, she sat down and started milking. Soon, the metal pail was full of warm frothy milk.

"Hannah," Annie called "where in tarnation have you got to now?"

"I'm in the hay loft, Granny, there's a blanket and backpack up here."

"I slept there last night," Caroline interjected. "That's what I want to talk to you about."

"Hannah, you come down from there and take this milk into the kitchen for me."

Hannah quickly climbed down the ladder and took the pail from Annie.

"Mind you don't spill any," Annie said. "I need it all as we're almost out of butter."

Hannah left the barn, humming quietly.

Annie slowly stood up, massaging her lower back with her hands. "These old bones aren't as limber as they used to be."

"Grandpa and Pete say the same thing."

Annie chuckled, bolted the latch to Blossom's stall and then headed outside.

When they arrived at the kitchen, Caroline noticed that Hannah had already started separating the cream. Annie helped her with the chore, and when they were finished, she placed her hand on the young girl's shoulder. "Go to the root cellar and bring me some eggs and bacon. We'll do the churning after breakfast."

Hannah nodded and left. Annie placed a piece of cheesecloth over the top of the container holding the cream then shuffled over to the table and sat down. She gestured for Caroline to sit down opposite her. "Now, sounds like you have something mighty important to talk about."

Caroline cleared her throat and then looked directly at Annie. "I was wondering if I could stay here for a while."

Annie took her bifocals off and wiped them with the bottom of her apron. She put them back on, pushing them higher on her nose. She stood, walked over to the cupboard and took out a mug. There was a pot of coffee sitting on the back burner of the stove. Annie poured a cup and returned to the table.

"Whyn't you tell me what this is all about?"

"I've run away from home."

"Now, what could be so terrible that you felt you had to run away from your family?"

"It's Grandpa, he's so hard to live with."

Annie nodded and took a sip of coffee.

"He says I can't see my friends anymore, which is so unfair."

Annie listened patiently, still saying nothing.

"He says I'm too young to date and now he's forbidden me to see Scott ever again."

"Who might this Scott be?"

"He goes to the same school that I do. His sister, Suzanne is my best friend."

"I'm thinking maybe Scott would be your beau?"

Caroline stopped talking and stared at Annie, at first not sure what she meant.

"Oh, you mean boyfriend?"

"That's what I said, your beau."

"He's not really my beau. He hasn't asked me to go steady or anything like that."

"Go steady to where?"

"You know, to be his girlfriend. He hasn't even given me his ring yet."

"Well, there you go, girl," Annie replied, slapping the palm of her hand on the table. "Your Grandpa's just being hard headed cause he feels you're much too young to get hitched."

Caroline shook her head, trying to wrap her mind around what Annie was saying.

"Do you mean get married?"

"Surely, girl. When a man gives you a ring, don't mean anything else."

"Annie, I don't think you understand. Scott wants to date me. You know go to mixed parties and maybe a movie show sometimes. But we're much too young to be thinking about getting married."

"Now, you're being sensible."

Caroline felt like laying her head down on the table and crying. How did this conversation get so confusing?

"It sounds as if your Grandpa's protecting you from making the wrong decision."

Caroline realized that Annie would not have understood anything she was told about her relationship with Scott, because her beliefs were probably even more out-dated than Grandpa's.

"He's going to sell Ebony."

"Land sakes, child, now why would he want to do that?"

"Because he's mean and despicable."

Annie leaned forward and placed her hand on top of Caroline's. "I can't believe your granddaddy would sell your horse unless he had a good reason."

"He says we need the money and that we might lose the ranch."

"Times is hard everywhere, child. Sometimes, we have to make tough decisions to survive."

"It's his entire fault. If he had taken better care of the ranch, we wouldn't be losing it."

"Now, you have no call to talk about your granddaddy that way. It ain't respectful."

Caroline sensed Annie's anger. "I'm sorry. I guess I'm just upset. The thought of losing Ebony is unbearable."

"One of the first lessons a body's got to learn is that life ain't always fair."

Caroline lowered her head and stared sullenly at the table top.

"You can stay for the day," Annie said, as she stood up and placed her mug on the counter. "But you have to go home first thing in the morning and settle things with your granddaddy."

It wasn't the answer Caroline expected to hear. She was hoping that Annie would have taken her side.

Caroline followed the elderly woman out the back door and onto the stoop.

"Now, where in tarnation has that child disappeared to?"

"I'm here Granny, in the root cellar," Hannah answered in a muffled voice.

"You put away your writing book and attend to your chores."

Hannah's face peeked around the heavy wooden door. She was grinning and her eyes sparkled in merriment. "Here's the bacon and eggs," she said, holding up the basket.

"Bring them in and start frying the bacon. I'm going to put Caroline to work in the barn, and then after breakfast, I'll get her to help me with the chimney."

Hannah scooted past them in the doorway and put the basket on the counter. Annie shook her head and laughed softly. "That child always has her nose buried in a book, or she's writing in that journal of hers. I don't have much learning, seeing as I only got a grade four education. I'm teaching Hannah her letters and how to read some, and she's right quick at picking up things on her own."

"Doesn't Hannah go to school?'

"Ain't one close enough, she gets mighty lonely at times not having chillun her own age to play with. Guess that's why she writes in her journal so much. She keeps it hidden in the root cellar in that purty sunflower canister, except nobody's supposed to know it's there."

Caroline chuckled. "I hide my journal under my bed, although I don't imagine there's anyone really interested in reading it but me."

"I guess that's why you put your personal thoughts down on paper, too. You're just lonely, like Hannah."

Caroline did not answer Annie, but followed her to

the barn. When they were inside, Annie pointed to the pens. "When you're finished mucking the stalls you can feed the livestock. By then breakfast should be ready. "

Caroline sighed deeply. Seems like no matter where she was, she couldn't get away from doing chores.

Chapter 13
Clogged Fireplace and a Boy on a Buckskin Horse

When Caroline had finished in the barn, she returned to the house. Annie was setting out platters of bacon, eggs and baking soda biscuits on the table. Although Caroline had already eaten, she found she was still hungry. Maybe her appetite was finally coming back.

After breakfast, Annie left the kitchen. Hannah began to clear the table and when Caroline started to help her, Hannah shook her head and pointed in the direction of the hallway.

Caroline heard rummaging at the far end of the corridor and walked in that direction.

"If that's you, Caroline, I'm here in the parlour."

For some reason, Caroline was not surprised to hear Annie call the living room a parlour.

Annie was spreading an old soiled blanket on the floor around the base of the fireplace. There was a long-handled broom leaning against the sofa.

"I asked that grandson of mine to clean the hearth afore he left, but he was so excited about going on his first round-up, he plumb forgot. There's something stuck in there and I don't want to take a chance on a fire starting in the chimney."

Caroline leaned over and looked inside. "I remember when Grandpa cleaned our fireplace last year. Turned out a bird had built a nest in it and we had baby swallows flying all over the house."

Annie took the broom and poked it into the chimney. Caroline stepped way back, in case it turned out to be something more than a bird. It wasn't unusual for hornets to build nests in the flues, or for skunks or raccoons to take up residence.

"I can't reach it. It must be higher up. You're going

to have to climb upon the roof and try from the other end."

Caroline looked at Annie in disbelief. "But it's two stories up."

"There's a trap door in the bedroom upstairs. My son built it a few years back. He's a real good carpenter. Don't worry, it works slick as a whistle."

Caroline followed Annie out of the room and up the stairs. They headed towards a bedroom at the end of the hallway, which was located directly above the living room. Annie entered a closet on the far wall. A square had been cut into the ceiling and there was a door covering it with a latch that locked from the inside. A ladder was leaning against the wall and Annie moved it over and fit it into two grooves carved into the moulding surrounding the opening. Caroline was impressed at the ingenuity of the design.

Apprehensively, she climbed the ladder, unlocked the latch, and pushed the trapdoor with both her hands. It lifted upwards without making a sound. She pulled herself through the hole and sat on the roof, the chimney was directly in front of her.

She shimmied over and carefully stood up, holding tightly to the edge of the chimney. Caroline peeked inside, but it was just as dark from this end.

"Here's the broom," Annie said from below. Caroline reached over and took the handle.

"How did I get myself into this?" she muttered quietly to herself.

"You find anything?" Annie asked.

Caroline shoved the broom into the chimney and it hit something solid. "There's something in there, but I don't know what it is."

"I'm going downstairs to the parlour. Wait a few seconds afore you do anything."

"Yes, ma'am." Caroline answered.

She heard Annie's muffled footsteps as she walked across the bedroom floor. When she thought Annie would have reached the front room, she shoved the broom handle down as hard as she could. Suddenly the object gave way. It fell down the flue and landed with a thud two floors below. Caroline jumped back, coughing as the black soot covered her face and clothing.

Suddenly, the delicate scent of lilacs drifted upwards. Caroline felt lightheaded and she quickly grabbed the edge of the chimney. The branches of the tall trees surrounding the house began to ripple, and the walls of the barn on the far side of the yard appeared to be moving. Caroline closed her eyes and took a deep breath. When she opened them, everything had returned to normal. Being so high up must have made her dizzy.

Working her way back to the trapdoor, she threw the broom inside, and then climbed onto the top rung of the ladder. She lowered the cover and pushed the bolt back into place.

When Caroline reached the floor, she unhooked the ladder and leaned it against the wall. Then she strolled into the bedroom.

The walls were covered with photographs and she casually looked at them as she walked by. Suddenly, she stopped dead in her tracks. The picture directly in front of her was identical to the one Grandpa had hanging on the wall in his bedroom. She remembered him telling her it was taken when he was twelve years old. He was sitting on a buckskin horse and she recognized the barn in the background.

She tore around the room, looking at the rest of the photos. There was a family portrait of a middle aged man standing demurely behind a beautiful woman with blonde hair. A younger Hannah was sitting on her lap and the same boy was standing next to her, his hand resting lightly on her shoulder. Annie was seated next to the woman.

Caroline couldn't tear her eyes away from the woman. Why did she look so familiar? She shook her head in confusion, turned and walked slowly down the stairs as if in a trance. She entered the living room and stepped towards Annie, who was holding the soiled blanket in her arms.

"Can you believe it was a squirrel's nest? It was full of acorns and seeds."

When Caroline did not answer, Annie raised her head. Seeing the look on her face, she set the blanket down on the floor and led Caroline over to the sofa.

"Land sakes child, sit down, you're as white as a ghost."

"Who's the boy in the pictures upstairs? He's sitting on a buckskin horse, and he's also in the family portrait standing next to a blond woman holding Hannah."

"Why that's Joseph, my grandson. Why do you ask?"

"My Grandpa's name is Joseph, and he has the same picture in his bedroom at home. When was it taken?"

"'Bout three years ago," Annie replied, sitting down next to Caroline. "The people in the portrait are my son Eric, his wife Sarah, and their children, Hannah and Joseph."

"Annie, what's your last name?"

"It's Lindstrom, same as yours."

"Why didn't you tell me we had the same name?"

"It weren't time to tell you, chil'."

Suddenly, a feeling of trepidation swept over Caroline. "That's the second time you've told me that. Annie, what's going on? What year is this?"

The old woman sighed then looked down at her hands.

"Annie, please, what year is it?" Caroline asked again, trying desperately to keep the hysteria out of her voice.

"It's 1902."

The last thing Caroline remembered was the room

spinning and Annie reaching out to her as she slid off the sofa.

Chapter 14
Annie's Revelation and Sarah's Vision

Caroline opened her eyes. Annie was sitting next to her, dabbing her forehead with a wet cloth. Hannah was standing behind the sofa, wringing her hands and staring down at Caroline.

"Look, Granny, she's waking up."

"Are you feeling better now?" Annie asked Caroline as she placed the cloth in a bowl of water sitting on the floor next to the sofa.

Caroline nodded and slowly sat up.

"Hannah, why don't you gather the eggs?" Annie said, looking up at her granddaughter. "Caroline and I'll finish cleaning up in here."

Hannah reached over and patted Caroline lightly on her head. She smiled at Annie, and turned and left the room.

At first, Caroline wasn't sure what to say. She reached over and took Annie's hands in her own. "Annie you told me the year was 1902."

"Yes, chil', I did."

"I live in the year 1956 with my Grandpa, whose name is Joseph Lindstrom. How can this possibly be?"

Annie stood up slowly and walked over to the window. She stared outside for the longest time. "Come with me, I want to show you something," she said, as she turned and left the room. She headed towards the stairs leading to the second floor.

Caroline followed Annie into the back bedroom and over to the picture of the family portrait hanging on the wall. "Look at Sarah and tell me what's you see."

Caroline stood closely behind Annie and stared at the photograph. Her heart pounded erratically, she gasped, and stepped back in shock. "It's her, the woman in my dreams, and she's wearing my locket. That's why she looked so familiar."

"It's Sarah's locket, Caroline. I seen it around your neck the first time you come here," Annie said quietly. "That's how come I knowed for sure who you was."

"Are you trying to tell me that this locket brought me back to this time and place?"

"The locket was just a way of gettin' you here, but it was Sarah who made it happen."

Annie shook her head in disbelief. She hugged herself tightly, then walked over to the bed and sat down.

"I'm sorry, none of this makes sense."

"Sarah was a very special woman, she saw things afore they happened."

"You mean she was psychic?" Caroline asked.

"If you mean she had certain powers, then, yes. Just my son and I knew and we never talked about it in front of strangers. People have funny notions 'bout things they don't understand."

"Yes, I know," Caroline replied quietly.

"After Hannah was born, Sarah became real sick. It was scarlet fever and she never really got better. When Hannah was six and Joseph was twelve, she got sick again, and we knowed she wasn't going to make it. Her heart was too weak. The day 'afore she died, she called me into her room and had me close the door. She made me promise to never tell anyone what she was going to say. Her locket was sitting on her night table and she picked it up and handed it to me. She told me it was to go to Hannah and she was to store it in her sunflower canister.

Then she told me something I wished I'd never heard. She said something terrible was going to happen to the family. I never for a moment doubted her, so I asked her to tell me what it was so that I could stop it. I remember the sadness on her face and the grief in her eyes. She told me that trying to change the future could affect many people's lives and not for the better. And no matter what I might try to do, things would still come out the same because you can't change a person's fate. She told me that Joseph would become very angry and bitter and would carry his guilt with him for the rest of his life and the only person who could heal him was someone close to him, someone who would be born in the future. It would be up to that person to set things right and to make him whole again."

Caroline felt the tears flowing down her face. She wiped them away with the back of her sleeve. Annie came and sat down beside her and Caroline rested her head on her shoulder. "I suppose that person you're talking about is me?"

"The truth is buried in the past," Annie whispered, "but the answer lies in the future."

Caroline gasped loudly then covered her face with her hands. "I remember everything now, that's what Sarah said to me in my dreams."

"It were her way of letting you know it were time to set things right."

"Then you must be my great, great grandmother," Caroline said, looking into Annie's eyes, "and Hannah is my great aunt?"

"I reckon that's so," Annie nodded.

"There are so many loose ends, so much I don't understand. If Hannah inherited the locket, then how did I end up with it?"

"That's why Sarah had Hannah hide it in her sunflower canister."

"I got it from my Grandma Lindstrom when she died, so I guess Grandpa must have found it and given it to her."

"More'n likely," Annie replied.

"Am I to tell Grandpa about all of this? If I do, he'll think I'm crazy or making up stories."

"Won't serve no purpose telling him anything atall."

"Maybe I should meet Grandpa, I mean Joseph, when he gets back and talk to him here?"

Annie shook her head solemnly. "I'm sorry Caroline, you can't do that. It's important you don't meet or talk to him about nothing. You might say or do something that would change both your lives. It's too dangerous. And promise me you won't say nothing to Hannah. The same thing goes for her."

Caroline nodded solemnly. She pulled away from Annie and stood up and walked over to the photograph. She stared a long time at Sarah's image.

"You see the sameness 'tween you and Sarah, don't you?" Annie asked as she walked over and stood behind Caroline.

"What do you mean?"

"Look closely. You have the same face, the same color of hair, even the same eyes. I noticed it the minute I laid eyes on you."

"I guess that's why she seems so familiar to me, like I've known her my entire life."

"I'm surprised your granddaddy never talked about her to you, he was right close to Sarah and took her death real hard."

"The only person he talks to is Uncle Pete. They've been friends forever. "

"Who might Uncle Pete be?"

"Pete Morgan. He's not my real uncle, but he lives with us and helps us around the ranch."

"He was your Grandpa's best friend."

"He still is," Caroline said with a smile.

"He showed up when he was maybe ten or eleven years old. Joe found him in the hay loft where he was hiding. He was scrawny as a starving coyote and his clothes were hanging on him in tatters. Joe took a liking to him and snuck grub and an old horse blanket out to him. Course, Eric heard them moving around in the loft one day and that's how we met Pete. Joe wanted Pete to stay with us, said he'd help with the chores, and would sleep in the barn. But we had to say no, 'cause there weren't enough food to feed another body. Told him he had to go back to his family. That night he disappeared as quietly as when he showed up."

Caroline sat quietly, intrigued by Annie's tale.

"'Bout a month later, he comes riding into the yard on a half wild mustang and he's leading two others behind him."

Caroline grinned, picturing Pete galloping up to the corral and surprising the family with his reappearance.

"That's how I got Ebony," Caroline said. "Pete found him running with a herd of wild mustangs."

"Don't surprise me atall. That boy knowed more about horses than most growed men did."

"I'm sorry I interrupted, Annie. Please continue with your story."

"Well, that young lad jumped off that horse, walks over to Eric, and hands over the two horses. Then he says, 'These are good horses and you can make a good trade for them.' Dang if he didn't blow all of us over."

"So, Eric took the horses and let Pete stay?"

"Not at first. Eric was right grateful for the offer, cause them horses would fetch a good price, and would surely help us out. He handed them ponies back to Pete and told him that he should take them back to his family, as they could use the food as much as anyone. Times were tough, especially for the tribes. There was lots of sickness and hunger everywhere."

"Pete never said nothing," Annie continued, "but Joe stepped up and told us that Pete's parents and his brothers and little sister had all died of the smallpox, and that almost everyone from his tribe was dead. Dang if you could have heard a pin drop, it was so quiet. That's when I stepped in and decided that Pete was going to stay. One skinny little boy weren't going to eat us out of house and home and Joseph's bedroom was big enough for two boys to bunk in."

"He never told us that story," Caroline said quietly.

"Pete ain't much for talking. He wouldn't have said nothing to us about his family if Joe hadn't spoke up. Reckon Pete figured he owed Joe a whole lot, finding him a home and all. Them two boys are as different as night and day, yet they were always together and somehow managed to get along."

"Grandpa can be pretty ornery but Pete is just the opposite. If it wasn't for him, Grandpa and I would have killed each other years ago."

"'Pears to me, stubbornness and having a quick temper must run in the family," Annie said as she walked over to the door. "Come along, we have to get supper started."

Caroline followed Annie down the stairs. For once, she did not have anything to say.

Chapter 15
A Song from the Fifties and Hannah's Journal

Caroline was famished and enjoyed Annie's wholesome meal. Dessert was apple pie. She wished she could get her pie crust to be as flaky, and when she asked Annie what her secret was, Annie said lots of years of practice and a strong rolling pin arm. Caroline laughed and Hannah giggled.

Soon, the dishes were cleared away and everyone went and sat in the parlour. Annie started a fire, pulling her rocking chair closer to the warmth.

"Sure do feel good on these old bones," she muttered. "I thank you, Caroline for helping me clean the chimney. We ain't had a fire since the men left and sometimes it gets mighty chilly at night. My new wood stove in the kitchen works real dandy, but there ain't anything homier than a fire burning in the hearth."

"You're welcome," Caroline answered pensively. She was deep in thought, trying to sort out everything Annie had just told her. She was still finding it hard to believe. Time travel was something you did not discuss with people. It was like telling someone you believe in ghosts and Caroline was glad she had not discussed her dreams about Sarah with anyone. She began to understand the discrepancy in the weather and why the flowers never changed and why the men were away working. Even though months had passed in the future, Annie and Hannah were in the same time frame as Caroline's first visit. Her mind reeled, trying to make sense of everything.

What was she supposed to find out? What was the terrible disaster that was going to befall the family? The more Caroline thought about it, the more her anxiety increased. Maybe something was going to happen to Grandpa or Joseph as she had come to think of him in this time and place?

"Caroline, do you play the piano?" Annie asked, interrupting her thoughts.

"Yes, ma'am," Caroline replied. "My grandmother taught me."

"Why don't you play us a tune?"

Caroline walked over to the old upright and sat down on the wooden bench. For a few seconds, her mind went blank. What were some of the tunes sung in 1902? Suddenly a song popped into her head. She began playing *Rock Around the Clock* and hoped it wouldn't sound too risqué. Hannah immediately jumped up and started dancing around the room while Annie clapped her hands and stomped her foot on the floor. Caroline played it over and over, until Hannah collapsed in an exhausted heap on the floor.

"Land sakes that were a lot of fun," Annie cackled gleefully, as she stood up and walked over to the window. She pulled the lace curtain aside and peeked outside. "Time for bed, it's getting dark."

Caroline followed Annie and Hannah out of the room and up the stairs. "You can bunk in with Hannah," Annie said to Caroline. "Don't talk too late, five o'clock comes early."

Caroline was startled by the comment, suddenly feeling homesick. She watched Annie's bowed figure walk slowly down the hallway. She reminded her so much of Grandpa, his mannerisms and the way he talked. Why hadn't she noticed it before?

Caroline followed Hannah into her bedroom. The young girl walked over to her night table and struck a match, lighting a candle that was sitting next to a vase of lilacs. Caroline's pack was lying on the bed.

"I brought your things in from the barn," Hannah said.

Caroline thanked the young girl. She unpinned her

silver broach and laid it on the night table. Then she began to unbutton her shirt and Hannah shyly turned her back. She waited until Caroline announced she was changed before she turned around. Hannah looked at her for the longest time, and then reaching over, she touched Caroline's pyjamas.

"How come you're wearing long johns? Don't you have a night gown?"

Remembering Annie's comment about not letting Hannah know who she was, Caroline hesitated before she answered.

"Um, yes, but I wear these when I'm travelling. They're warmer and easier to pack."

Hannah seemed satisfied with Caroline's explanation. She reached under her pillow and pulled out her journal.

"I write in my journal every night, and then I hide it in the root cellar during the day. I wrote about your last two visits."

"You did? What did you say? I mean, do you mind telling me what you said."

"Sure."

Hannah jumped up on the bed and patted a spot for Caroline to sit. When the two girls were settled, Hannah raised her knees and propped up her journal.

"I'm not real good at writing yet."

Caroline smiled and patted Caroline's hand. "I'm sure you've done a wonderful job."

"Caroline come to visit us today. She was riding a black horse, and he was really skittish. His name is Ebony. Granny played her geetar and we sang lots of songs. I showed her our root cellar and my sunflower tin. We had lemonaid and sugar cookies."

"Hannah, that's wonderful." Caroline said, not pointing out the spelling errors. "And you read very well."

Hannah's face lit up with the compliment. "I wrote

some more. Do you want me to read it?"

"Oh, yes, please."

"*Caroline came to see us again the next day. She said she could not stay away. I think Caroline is funny. I showed her Eva and Alice, and we played for a while in the garden. She did not stay for supper cause she had to go home and feed her grandpa. I hope Caroline comes back soon, cause I really like her.*"

Caroline smiled fondly at the young girl. Hannah reached over and took a pencil from the top of her night table. She lowered her head and started writing. Caroline rolled over to the far side of the bed and crawled under the quilt, pulling it up over her shoulders.

Hannah scribbled for a few minutes, and Caroline closed her eyes.

"Caroline, how do you spell chimney?"

Caroline spelled it out for her. "Are you telling about Annie and me cleaning out the fireplace?"

"Yes, and about Granny finding a squirrel's nest and about starting a fire and you playing such a happy song."

"That's wonderful. When you're finished don't forget to blow out the candle."

"I'm all done. I sure am glad you come back to visit us again. I like you, Caroline."

"And I like you, Hannah, very much."

It wasn't long before Hannah was sound asleep. Caroline's mind raced over the events of the day. She stared out the window at the flickering stars. Even though she was still angry at Grandpa, she knew she had to go home tomorrow, and when the time was right, she would come back here again when she found out what she had to do to make things right.

After breakfast the next morning, Caroline offered to milk Blossom for Annie, who heartily agreed. After she had carried the pail of milk to the kitchen, she joined

Hannah in the chicken coop and chatted with the young girl while she fed the chickens and gathered the eggs. Caroline was wondering who was taking care of her chores back at the ranch, when she suddenly remembered that when she returned to the future, no time would have passed since she left there, except for her travelling time up and down the mountain.

When Hannah had finished her chores, the two girls strolled back to the house. Caroline looked around the farmyard. The neat house, red painted barn, tidy flower beds and garden reflected the family's pride in their ownership. She wondered why Grandpa did not feel the same way about their place and had let it fall into disrepair after he had inherited it from Eric. Could it have something to do with what had happened to the family? Although she did not know much about running a ranch, she understood that having no mortgage, and growing their own food, should have put them financially ahead of most of the struggling ranchers they knew.

"Can't you stay a little longer?" Hannah asked sadly. "Pa, Pete and Joseph will be back tomorrow or the next day, and I want you to meet them."

"I'd love to meet them, but I've been gone a long time and my family will be worried about me," Caroline answered.

All too soon, it was time to leave. Caroline fetched her backpack and reluctantly strolled to the barn. Hannah and Annie followed closely behind.

Soon, Ebony was saddled and Caroline led him outside. She stopped at the corral and Hannah ran over and hugged her tightly. "Bye, Caroline, I'll miss you."

"Goodbye, Hannah, you be good now."

A feeling of foreboding hit Caroline and she felt a shiver run down her arms and back.

Annie stepped forward and took Caroline's face in her hands. "You take care of yourself, girl."

Caroline felt a lump in her throat. She grabbed Annie and gave her a hug. "I'll come back as soon as I can, I promise."

"Caroline, there's something else I has to tell you," Annie whispered in her ear. "Sarah warned me that you can only travel back in time no more than four times, and each time you come back, the connection gets weaker and weaker. This is your third time, so you only have one visit left. Please remember that and we'll see you again when the time is right."

Caroline climbed up on Ebony's back and rode across the yard. When she got to the mountain ash, she turned and waved. Annie and Hannah were still standing next to the corral.

Caroline steered Ebony into the trees and experienced the usual tingling in her arms and legs. Ebony picked up his speed, anxious to get away from the gateway, or whatever it was they passed through to go back in time. She knew that animals had a sixth sense about this sort of thing and it explained why he was so nervous each time they passed through.

At first, she was startled to find that it was no longer mid-morning. It was dark and the moonlight radiated through the trees, outlining the trunks and branches. She wondered if she had come back on a different day, but quickly dismissed that idea, as that had not been the pattern regarding her previous visits.

Ebony trotted over to the main trail. The temperature was considerably warmer. Caroline retrieved her flashlight from her saddle bag and turned it on. She rode cautiously, keeping a sharp lookout for roots and rocks. When she arrived at the fork, she dismounted and led Ebony down the steep path. Going downhill was a lot more precarious than climbing up.

Finally, she arrived at the base of Eagle Mountain. The outline of the ranch house and the outbuildings came into view. She led Ebony over to the barn. He whinnied when he recognized the familiar surroundings and walked directly to his stall. She took off his saddle, quickly rubbed him down, and gave him fresh water and hay.

She crept around to the back of the house and walked up the porch steps. She opened the door, hung her jacket up, and walked into the kitchen and across the floor to the back stairs. It was unnaturally quiet. The only sounds she heard was the ticking of the grandfather clock in the living room and the creaking of a floor board settling in the old house.

Arriving at her bedroom, she leaned heavily against the door, taking a deep breath. She shoved her pack under her bed. It was warm in the room, and she opened the window wide, letting in a cool breeze.

"Caroline, are you awake?" Grandpa called from down the hall.

"I just opened my window," Caroline answered, her heart beating rapidly. "It's so hot in here."

"You better get some shut eye. You have to get up in a few hours."

"Yes, Grandpa," she said.

Caroline sat down heavily on the edge of her bed. She looked over at her clock, the time was 12:45 a.m. A little over two hours had passed since she had left, which was approximately the amount of time it had taken her to reach Annie's place and to get back again. She did not try to understand how the time frame worked, and wondered again if there could have been a possibility she might have come back in the future, or for that matter returned to some other time in her past. If she spent any more time dwelling on it, she would go crazy.

She took off her jeans and shirt, and curled up on her bed in her underclothes. Last night she slept in her pyjamas and woke up to a cool, misty morning. Now, a few hours later, she was trying to fall asleep in stifling heat.

Caroline rolled over and closed her eyes.

She tossed and turned all night, replaying everything that had happened. It wasn't until early morning when she suddenly realized she had left her silver brooch lying on Hannah's night table. How did Scott's mother get it? She probably would never find out, as it was quite conceivable she would never talk to Scott again, and at least she wouldn't have to try and explain to him where she had lost it.

Chapter 16
Camping Out and Questioning Pete

The next morning, Caroline could barely keep her eyes open. She went about her chores, exhausted from her sleepless night.

When breakfast was over, she cleared the table and then poured water into the sink. She picked up a mug and washed it in the soapy water. She stared out the window, sighed deeply, and rewashed the mug a second time.

Caroline suddenly realized the room was quiet and Grandpa and Pete had stopped talking. She turned to face them and saw they were watching her curiously.

"I'm just tired. I didn't sleep very well last night. It was too hot."

"It was mighty hot in the bunkhouse, too," Pete remarked. "I think tonight I'm going to sleep outside. Anyone care to join me?"

Caroline nodded and looked at Grandpa. During the summer, if it got too hot in the house to sleep, they would haul their sleeping bags out to the fire pit and camp out under the stars. Pete always started a fire, he would play his harmonica and they would talk for hours. Sometimes, Grandpa would join them and sometimes he didn't, depending on his mood. Shaking his head, he took a sip of his coffee and answered, "I have a perfectly good bed, why would I want to sleep on the hard ground?"

The day went slowly. Caroline would stop in the middle of whatever she was doing and would stare off into the distance. If Grandpa happened to see her, he would quietly complain about her day dreaming and her chores not getting done. Caroline would follow his retreating figure with her eyes, surprised that his muttered comments did not bother her more.

That night she made a supper of cold ham, buns,

potato salad and raw carrots from the garden. Grandpa grumbled throughout the meal, commenting that a hardworking man needed more than rabbit food to keep him going, however he ate everything on his plate. Caroline did not want to start the stove and heat up the kitchen any more than it already was. She made a tall pitcher of lemonade and filled glasses for everyone. She and Pete sat outside on the porch, enjoying a breeze blowing down from Eagle Mountain. Grandpa had strolled into the living room to read his cattle reports. The lemonade, along with a plateful of gingersnap cookies, soon disappeared.

She yawned, trying hard to keep from falling asleep. She wondered how long it would take her to straighten out the change in her sleep pattern.

"Well, I reckon it's time to call it a day," Pete drawled. "Why don't you go get your sleeping bag and I'll meet you over by the fire pit?"

Caroline carried the glasses and the empty pitcher to the kitchen. She placed them in the sink, deciding that the morning would be soon enough to wash them. Then she went to her bedroom and dug out her sleeping bag from under her bed. She quickly changed into her pyjamas and put on her robe.

She barrelled down the steps, barely missing Grandpa climbing up. He did not say anything and waited until she had gone past before he continued to his room.

Caroline ran across the yard, with Rusty running closely behind, nipping playfully at her heels. She giggled and patted the playful dog on his head.

She rolled out her sleeping bag next to the fire and crawled inside. Pete already had his out and was lying on top, peacefully smoking a cigarette.

The chirping of crickets serenaded them and a coyote yipped a short distance away. Rusty growled under his breath, but was too comfortable to move.

"Uncle Pete," Caroline said. "How long have you

known Grandpa?"

"Since I was a young lad."

"Then you must have known his family?"

"Shore did."

"How come Grandpa never talks about them?"

"They have been gone a long time. No sense dwelling on it, I guess."

"I know he grew up here on this ranch with his father but he's never mentioned anyone else in his family. What happened to his mother?"

"She died of scarlet fever when he was twelve. How come you're asking me about them?"

"I often wonder about my relatives, you know, where I came from, that sort of thing."

"Hmmm. I guess we all get curious about our kin, sooner or later."

"Was Grandpa an only kid, like me?"

Pete inhaled deeply then he tossed his cigarette butt into the fire.

"No, he had a sister. Her name was Hannah."

"What happened to her?"

"She died when she was very young, along with their grandmother. It was a terrible tragedy and your Grandpa never got over it."

"What do you mean? What happened?" Caroline asked, trying to keep the panic out of her voice.

"I think I'll let your Grandpa answer that question. If he knew I was talking to you about them, he'd be purely rankled at me."

"Pete, you know he won't say anything to me."

"It ain't my place to tell you. We better call it a night, you look pretty wiped," Pete said, tossing some more wood on the fire.

"Goodnight, Pete," Caroline said.

She closed her eyes, pretending to be asleep. For the longest time, she thought about what Pete had told her.

The tragedy had to do with Annie and Hannah. How did they die? If she only knew what had happened, she could go back and warn them. Then she remembered Annie's admonition about interfering with fate.

Caroline wished she had someone to talk to about what she was going through, yet she knew that no-one would believe a word she said. She was on her own and she unquestionably knew time was running out.

Chapter 17
Anger and Despair

Caroline watched Pete closely for the next few days, hoping to catch him alone so that she could question him again. She knew there would be no sense in approaching Grandpa, because he was still angry at her, and spent most of his time in the barn or outside working on the old tractor. Whenever she had the chance, she would scrounge through cupboards or boxes stored in the spare rooms, but she had not found anything that gave any information about Grandpa's past.

An opportunity came at the end of the week while Grandpa and Pete were working together in the barn. Caroline raced upstairs and snuck into Grandpa's bedroom. His window looked down on the front yard, so she would see if either he or Pete decided to return to the house.

The first thing that caught her eye was the same photograph hanging in Annie's bedroom, the one of Grandpa sitting on Buck. Caroline looked quickly around the room. There was Grandpa's huge over-sized bed, the armoire in the far corner, the shelves full of books, the roll top desk buried under stacks of papers, envelopes and pamphlets. She casually scrutinized everything in view, but she dared not touch anything. If Grandpa knew she was in his bedroom, there would be no telling what he would do. Somehow she knew she would find nothing here. She had to be looking in the wrong place.

She left the room, closing the door quietly. She stood in the middle of the hallway, wondering where to look next. She walked quickly down the stairs, into the kitchen and over to the root cellar. She swung open the door, flicked on the light and walked slowly down the steps. When she got to the bottom, she stood for a few seconds, her heart pounding. She walked over to the far corner and stopped.

A wooden trunk was pushed up against the wall. It was covered by a tattered musty rug and a couple of wooden picture frames leaned precariously against its side. She recognized it as being the same trunk that was in Annie's root cellar.

She threw everything on the floor and then grabbed the latch. At first it wouldn't budge, but after a couple of tries, it finally gave way.

Inside were shoes and clothes smelling of mothballs and mildew. Pushing them aside, Caroline continued to dig. There at the bottom of the trunk was the sunflower canister. She reached in and removed it, making sure to close the trunk lid. Then she returned the clothes and frames where she had found them and quietly left.

Caroline raced upstairs to her bedroom and closed her door. She sat down on her bed, took a deep breath, and pried open the rusted lid of the canister. There was nothing inside except a stained red ribbon and Hannah's journal. Caroline opened it and began reading, not sure what she was looking for. There was nothing about her, or her visits. She tried to sort out the reasoning for this and finally decided that since she had not yet made things right as Sarah had foreseen, history had not been changed. Would that mean if she failed in her mission, everything that had transpired would never have happened? Would she even remember Annie and Hannah?

She returned the ribbon and the journal to the canister, then took the can and hid it under her bed.

The next morning, while Caroline was scrubbing the kitchen floors the telephone rang. She jumped up, answered it, and was delighted to hear Suzanne's voice on the other end.

"Mom had the baby," Suzanne said excitedly. "We have a little sister."

"That's so cool, what did you call her?"

"Grace after my Grandma."

"You must be very happy. I know how much you wanted a little sister."

"Yeah, she is pretty cute. Except now I have to take care of the Terrible Twosome so Mom can get some rest. Thank goodness we have a television set because *The Lone Ranger* and *Rin Tin Tin* keeps them busy and out of my hair."

"How is everyone?"

"Cool. Caroline, guess what? Wesley and I are jacketed."

"Oh, Suzanne, that's so keen."

"And I'm working at the soda shop."

Caroline congratulated her friend, trying not to sound envious. She was glad that Suzanne and Wesley were going steady. Everyone was moving ahead in their lives, while she was living hers in the past.

Suddenly, Suzanne said, "Did I tell you Wesley's dad bought him a car?"

"No, that's so neat."

"It's a 1950 Chevy and it runs great. We drive into Olds all the time and go shopping or to the drive-in movie. We saw James Dean in *Rebel without a Cause* on Saturday night. Oh, Caroline, he's so dreamy and the movie was so hep. I wish you could have been there."

For a moment the line went quiet.

"Suzanne, are you there?"

"Caroline, it's me, Scott."

She said nervously, checking around the kitchen to make sure she was alone. "How have you been?"

"Great, I heard what Suzanne told you. I have a job, too. I've been working for Mr. Mitchell."

"That's keen."

"Only during the week and then I spend the weekends helping Dad at the hardware store. I'm keeping Monty stabled at the Mitchell's for the summer and then

I'll bring him back when school starts."

"Mr. Mitchell's lucky to have you."

"That's what I keep telling him," Scott said, laughing at his own joke.

Caroline was pleased that Scott had found a job doing what he loved so much.

"I miss you," Scott said.

"I miss you, too," Caroline replied quietly. "I suppose you're dating lots of different girls now?"

"You're the only one for me. All they're interested in is makeup, clothes and James Dean or that new singer, Elvis Presley."

"Scott, you're so funny."

"Now that I'm working just a few miles away, I was wondering if it would be all right if I came over once in a while to see you."

"Maybe we can meet somewhere. If you phone me first, we can arrange something."

"That's great. I can't wait. Oh, by the way, is it true?"

Scott's voice had turned sober, and Caroline stiffened. "Is what true?" she said quietly.

"Wesley told me that his dad just bought Ebony today from your Grandpa. I told him he was crazy. You'd never sell Ebony."

Suddenly the screen door closed with a bang. Caroline spun around in shock. Grandpa was standing at the counter, glaring angrily at her. She did not know how long he had been listening to her.

"Who's on the phone?" he asked sharply.

Caroline gripped the receiver tightly in her hand.

"It's that Chalmers boy isn't it? I thought I told you he was off-limits to you, along with that sister of his."

"Caroline, what does your Grandpa mean?" Scott asked. "You never told me we weren't supposed to see each other."

"Hang up the phone, Caroline," Grandpa ordered.

Caroline stood rooted to the spot, trying to piece together what she had just heard.

"Scott just told me you sold Ebony to the Mitchells. Is it true?" she screamed.

"He had no right telling you that. I was going to talk to you about it tonight."

"Caroline, I'm sorry, I shouldn't have said anything," Scott said. Suddenly Grandpa slammed his fist on the counter. His face had turned a deep shade of red and his eyes glared angrily. "Hang up the phone, now," he ordered.

"Scott, I know I should have said something to you but I couldn't bear not seeing you again," Caroline choked, as she laid the receiver down, not waiting for Scott's answer. Now she had lost him for good.

She stared at her grandfather and the despair and anger she felt tore her apart. Any feelings she might have felt towards him these last few days disappeared. No matter what Annie had told her, as far as she was concerned Grandpa would never change. He would always be a mean, vindictive man.

Turning sharply, she raced up the back stairs and down the hallway. When she got to her bedroom, she threw herself across her bed.

Her decision had been made for her. Tomorrow she would go back to Annie's. If there was any way she could help her and Hannah, she planned on doing it. She did not care what the consequences would be and if she could work it out, she would never come back. She would stay with Annie forever.

She would take Ebony with her. Grandpa would have to find another way to save his precious ranch.

Chapter 18
An Argument and Hearing the Truth

Caroline tossed and turned, finally falling asleep in the early morning hours. She dragged herself out of bed and went downstairs to the kitchen to start breakfast. Pete was sitting at the table drinking a cup of coffee. Grandpa was nowhere to be seen. Caroline sat down heavily in the closest chair.

"Caroline," Pete said. "I'm sorry you had to find out about Ebony that way. I was hoping your grandpa would discuss it with you first before he did anything."

"Why should he change now, Pete? He always does what he wants."

"It wasn't something he wanted to do, it was something he had to do. Right now you're angry at him but hopefully one day you will understand why he did what he did."

"No, you're wrong Pete. I'm not angry at him, I hate him, and I'll never forgive him."

Pete shook his head sadly. He reached over and placed his hand on her shoulder, but Caroline shrugged it off. She stood up quickly and walked out of the room.

Upstairs in her bedroom, she packed her clothes, throwing in her jeans, shirts, socks, and underclothes. She did not take anything else, but she was sure Annie would have some of Sarah's old dresses around that would fit her. She secretly wished she had room to pack Grandma's quilt. Caroline realized she would be leaving this life forever and packed only what she would need.

She remained in her room until noon then went downstairs and fixed a quick lunch, but left it sitting on the table. It was a scorcher outside, so she drew the curtains and closed the windows and the back door, hoping it would help to keep the house cool.

She strolled down the hallway and went into the living room. Pete was sitting at the card table, staring solemnly at his checker board. He looked up in surprise when she entered. Caroline sat down opposite him. Shaking his head sadly, he moved one of the pieces.

Grandpa was sitting in his chair drinking a cup of coffee. She did not look at him and he said nothing to her.

For a while, the only sound in the room was the ticking of the clock. Then Caroline rose from her chair and went and stood behind Pete. Placing her hand on his shoulder, she said. "I think I'll go upstairs and read."

"Not much else a body can do in this heat."

"Your lunch is on the kitchen table. Good bye, Pete."

Pete turned his head and looked up at her. Caroline smiled at him and then she turned and left the room.

She lay on her bed, deciding that she would leave in a few hours. It would be hard on Ebony climbing Eagle Mountain in this heat and she had decided to wait until it had cooled down a little. Suddenly, she heard raised voices coming from below.

She crept out of her room and stopped when she got to the bottom of the stairs. She edged up next to the wall, keeping herself hidden from view. Grandpa and Pete were having an argument and they were talking about her.

"Why are you being so stubborn about this?" Pete asked angrily. Caroline was troubled as she was not used to hearing him raise his voice.

"I don't want to talk about it anymore," Grandpa replied. "You know how I feel about Caroline dating. She's only fourteen."

"She'll be fifteen in a few weeks, but that ain't the problem. She needs to be with friends her own age, not two old coots like us."

"You know why I won't let her meet with her friends. When she does, she's seeing that boy."

"Seeing Scott is only an excuse. What are you so afraid of? You can't hold onto her for the rest of her life, you have to let her grow up sometime."

"Pete, let up. This is none of your business. She's my granddaughter, not yours."

For a few seconds Pete did not answer. When he did his voice was strained. "Don't say it's not my business. I've helped raise that girl as much as you have, for that matter, probably more."

"What do you mean by that?"

"I'm the one she comes to when she's hurting and lately that's been happening a lot. You should have seen her face this morning when I tried to talk about Ebony."

"I had no choice, Pete, and you know it. Life can be harsh sometimes."

"You should have done what I suggested. Why didn't you talk to her about it before you went ahead and sold him? Caroline is pretty level-headed and she might have understood what had to be done. Instead, you sold him behind her back and you know that horse means more to her than anything she has."

"That boy had no right telling her anything."

"He had no idea that Caroline didn't know about Mitchell buying Ebony."

"If she had listened to me in the first place and stopped seeing him, then this wouldn't have happened. She's so stubborn."

"Caroline's not the only stubborn one around here. If you would let up once in a while, she wouldn't feel like she has to fight you for everything she wants. I've spent years trying to keep peace in this house and I'm getting mighty weary."

"No one asked you to butt in."

"No, they didn't, and it's time I stopped."

"Now you're talking nonsense."

"You'll lose that young girl for good, Joe. I know

what I'm talking about. When she looks at you, her eyes are full of anger and hate."

"Pete, this conversation is over."

"Actually, we should have had this talk a long time ago. You know this has nothing to do with Caroline, but everything to do with what happened years ago. You're afraid you'll lose her, just like you did Hannah and Annie."

Caroline gasped, putting her hand over her mouth. It was the first time Grandpa or Pete had ever mentioned their names.

"You've been carrying so much guilt on your shoulders for so many years, you've become hateful and mean," Pete continued.

A loud bang and the sound of glass shattering on a hard surface made Caroline jump. "I've told you to never bring that matter up," Grandpa yelled. "It's over and done with."

"No, it ain't. It's done, but it ain't over. When are you ever going to stop blaming yourself for what happened?"

"It's my fault they're dead and nothing can change that."

"It was an accident, a terrible senseless disaster."

"It wasn't an accident, if I had cleaned out that chimney like Granny asked, they wouldn't have died. The house wouldn't have burned to the ground, Annie would have lived for another twenty years, and Hannah would still be here."

Caroline felt as if she was falling into a deep hole. How could there have been a fire? She and Annie had cleaned out the chimney.

"It was never proven the fire started in the chimney," Pete answered wearily. "It could have started anywhere."

"I remember asking Pa that same question and, if you recall, he couldn't give me an answer then."

Caroline slumped against the wall, trying to catch her breath. She walked towards the front door, letting it slam behind her when she stepped outside. She raced across the yard, into the barn and over to Ebony's stall. She opened the gate, jumped on his back, and galloped out of the barn, grabbing his mane tightly in her fists.

Someone was standing on the front porch and Caroline realized it was Pete. He did not try to call her back, but stood watching her as she tore down the roadway. Then, he turned and walked back inside the house.

Chapter 19
Fire and a Sunflower Canister

Ebony galloped down the path, jumping over roots and avoiding low hanging branches. Caroline had never pushed him this hard before and the faithful horse never faltered. She leaned forward, putting as much of her weight as she could on his shoulders.

Finally, they arrived at the fork. Caroline slowed Ebony's pace. The strenuous climb and the heat were taking its toll on him. He was breathing heavily and his withers were drenched in sweat.

They were almost at the mountain ash. By now, the locket was warm and Caroline's arms and legs had started tingling. She urged Ebony through the bushes.

Ebony whinnied and stopped sharply. He reared and Caroline was flung forward. She wrapped her arms tightly around his neck, stopping herself from being thrown. She patted his neck, encouraging him to continue, but he snorted and spun around in terror.

Ebony would not go any farther. Caroline jumped down off his back. If she went through the gateway, she would never return and she would never see him again. It was one of the hardest decisions she had ever had to make. She laid her head on Ebony's neck and gave him a hug. Forcing back tears, she turned and walked past the mountain ash and into the meadow. She knew that when she did not return Ebony would eventually make his own way down the mountain and back to the barn. Mr. Mitchell would end up with Ebony after all, and Grandpa would be able to save the ranch.

Caroline froze, staring in disbelief. Flames were shooting out of the second story windows of the house. She raced across the yard and tore up the porch steps two at a time. She flung open the front door and entered, but there was no-one in sight.

"Annie, Hannah, where are you?" she shouted.

A terrified scream came from upstairs and Caroline recognized Hannah's voice. She ran up the stairwell but had only gone a few steps when she was forced to stop. The fire had already reached the top landing. She gasped when she was hit by a blast of hot air. She backed down the steps, raising her arms, shielding her face from the intense heat.

She raced down the hallway and into the kitchen. There was a water bucket sitting on the counter. She grabbed it, went over to the wood stove, and lifted the lid of the reservoir. It was half full of water, so she scooped as much of it as she could into the bucket, and then raced back to the stairs.

By now the fire had spread along the banister and was making its way down the walls. The wallpaper crackled and curled as the intense flames devoured everything in its path. Caroline flung the water on the blaze. It sputtered, but the roaring inferno continued on its relentless journey.

She ran back to the kitchen, praying in desperation. She filled the bucket again, taking the last of the water in the reservoir. She ran to the stairs and stopped. The blaze had made its way down to the main floor and was heading towards the parlour. She watched in horror as the lace curtains started to burn. Caroline backed slowly away, realizing there was nothing she could do. She had never felt so helpless in her life.

Suddenly, she heard the sound of horse's hooves. She threw the bucket on the floor, ran out the back door, and around the corner of the house. Three horsemen were galloping down the roadway and Caroline recognized Joseph astride the lead horse, with his father following closely behind. A lanky, dark haired boy around Grandpa's age was on the third horse and Caroline realized it had to be

Pete. Had they arrived in time to save Hannah and Annie?

She was just about to call and get their attention when she suddenly remembered Annie's dire warning about being seen. She pulled herself back behind the house and ran around to the far side, which allowed her a view of the front porch.

She watched as Grandpa jumped off his horse before it had come to a complete stop. He leaped up the front steps, grabbed the handle and yanked the door open. The flames shot out, and Eric grabbed him by his arms and pulled him back, yelling at him to stop.

"Quick, the back door," he shouted, pointing in that direction.

Caroline looked anxiously around. If they decided to come this way, she would be discovered. She had to find a place to hide.

Retracing her steps, she ran to the back and turned down the path heading towards the root cellar. The door was ajar, so she ducked inside just as Eric and the two terrified boys appeared around the corner of the house.

Caroline stood as far back as she could, hiding in the shadows, where she had a clear view of the burning house. Eric flung open the kitchen door, but was forced back by the overpowering smoke. Suddenly, a spine-chilling scream was heard from upstairs followed by silence.

Grandpa struggled with his father, as he tried to get into the house. Eric grabbed him around his waist, pulling him back, yelling over the roar of the fire, telling him they were too late, there was nothing they could do. The agony on Grandpa's face was almost more than Caroline could bear. She collapsed to the dirt floor, covering her face with her hands, sobbing uncontrollably.

The smoke drifted into the root cellar and Caroline coughed as it spiralled up the dirt walls. It did not take long for the wooden house to burn completely to the ground. For the longest time, the only sound that could be heard was the crackling of the dying flames. Then there was a deathly silence.

Caroline raised her head and peeked outside. Grandpa, Eric and Pete were huddled closely together, as if they were trying to keep each other from falling over. They stared in stunned silence at the smouldering remains of the house. The second floor had collapsed into the lower floor. The only thing recognizable was the kitchen stove lying at an angle on top of a pile of charred boards and debris. Everything else had been burned to cinders.

Caroline stood up shakily and staggered to the back of the cellar. She leaned against the potato bin. She had failed Annie; she had failed Hannah; and she had failed Sarah.

Angrily, she slammed her fist down onto her open palm, trying to make sense of Sarah's foretelling. Each time she had come through the gateway, she had returned to this particular place and time, so the answer must lie here. What was she missing?

All at once, the walls began to shift, as a wave of nausea hit her. At first, she thought it was the trauma of the fire but her locket was getting warm and the familiar tingling along her arms and legs made her realize what was happening. She remembered Annie's warning that each time she returned the link became weaker and weaker.

Suddenly, a soft glow filled the root cellar. It was radiating from Hannah's sunflower canister, which was sitting on top of the old trunk. Caroline slowly approached the tin, reached over and picked it up.

Her head started spinning and she leaned against the trunk, waiting for the dizziness to disperse.

She pried open the lid and looked inside. There were two photographs, a bright red ribbon, her silver horse broach, and Hannah's journal. She took the book out and opened it to the last entry.

Caroline went home today. She forgot her shiny horse broach. Granny gave me the pitcher of the whole family and the one of Joe riding Buck that was on the wall upstairs. I put them and Caroline's broach in my tin can to keep them safe. I better go its getting dark. I just membered I left the candle burning on my table in my bedroom. Granny will be mad at me. She's says I have the brains of a chicken. I think that's funny. Hannah Louisa Lindstrom.

"Oh, Hannah, Hannah," Caroline whispered, clasping the journal tightly against her chest, while the tears flowed down her face. Her grief was all the more intense as she realized it had been less than an hour ago that Hannah had written these very words. Caroline remembered that the table was next to the window and she could only assume the wind had blown the curtains into the flames and started the fire.

Caroline walked over to the entrance and peered outside. The sun was starting to set and the shadows of the trees reached across the yard. Grandpa, Eric, and Pete had wandered over to the lawn and were sitting on the ground under the scorched branches of a huge poplar. Grandpa's face and arms were black with soot and his tears had left streaks on his face, Eric was crying softly and Pete watched them stoically, hiding his emotions as he always did.

"It's my fault they're dead," Grandpa moaned.

"Stop it, Joseph. It was an accident," Eric said, shaking Grandpa's arm.

"No, it wasn't an accident. Granny asked me to clean the fireplace, but I was so excited about going on the cattle drive, I forgot all about it."

"You don't even know if that's what caused the fire, son."

"What else could it be?"

Eric couldn't answer. He hung his head in misery, staring at the ground.

It was then Caroline realized what her mission was. Grandpa must find Hannah's journal and he had to read it. Then and only then would he realize the fire was not his fault.

The light-headedness returned, reminding Caroline her time was running out. She needed to find somewhere to leave the book where it would be found. The answer came to her in a rush.

She stepped out of the cellar, turned left, then crouched behind the lilac hedge, thankful for the encroaching darkness. From her position, she had a broad view of the lawn, the trees, Eric and the distraught boys.

Creeping quietly along the length of the bushes, she arrived at her destination. Before her was the lattice, with Hannah's doll table and chairs underneath. She cautiously walked across the grass and hid behind the huge trunk of the old cottonwood. Dizziness overtook her and she felt the warmth of her locket against her chest. Caroline looked down and stared in disbelief. She could see right through her body. Her arms and legs were starting to disappear. She only had a few minutes left.

Reaching over, Caroline laid the canister on top of the table. She lifted her head and gasped in shock. Pete was watching her and, for a few seconds, they stared into each other's eyes. Caroline felt her strength disappearing and the pressure on her chest became heavier. She turned and started running, following the lilac bushes until she got to the root cellar. Then she ran towards the huge trees bordering the burned out shell of the house. Caroline was so exhausted she had difficulty making her feet move. Somehow, she realized that if she did not get to the gateway on time, she would not return to the future, and she would cease to exist here in the past.

Relief washed over her when she finally spied the mountain ash a few feet away.

Her locket had started to glow and was vibrating.

She leaned against the trunk of the tree, willing herself not to pass out.

She took one last look around. Pete was still watching her. He nodded and looked at the canister. Caroline lunged through the dense bush, her head spinning and her heart pounding. She fell heavily to the ground. Reaching inside her shirt, she groped for the locket, but it was not there. It had disappeared.

She lay on the forest floor, breathing heavily. A nearby bird chirped while a squirrel noisily chattered. She slowly sat up and looked around, surprised that everything looked the same when her own life felt as if it had ended.

A shuffling noise caught her attention. Ebony was standing a few feet away, not far from where she had left him. His withers were still wet from his strenuous run. He approached her and nudged her with his nose. Caroline stood up unsteadily, wrapping her arms around his neck, leaning against his strong muscular body.

Caroline climbed unsteadily onto Ebony's back and gently kneed the patient horse. She had never felt such intense sorrow. Laying her head on Ebony's neck she let the tears flow unheeded. Instinctively, she knew Pete would take the canister to Eric, they would find Hannah's journal and discover the truth.

The difference in the temperature reminded Caroline that it was July and still early in the afternoon. She allowed Ebony to walk at his own pace, letting him cool down after his strenuous climb.

Caroline's mind replayed what had just transpired. She remembered the searing flames racing down the stairwell, eating everything in its path. Hannah's screams echoed through her head, and even though she and Annie had died almost fifty years ago, to Caroline it had just happened.

When Ebony arrived at the fork, he automatically turned left, heading down the mountain. When he realized he was not far from the ranch, he picked up his speed. Caroline did not notice the root across the path until it was too late. Ebony tripped, then he reared, attempting to right himself.

The last thing she remembered before the world went black was falling toward the trunk of a huge pine tree next to the path.

Chapter 20

A Concussion and Good Advice

Caroline heard her name being called from a distance. She tried to open her eyes, but everything was out of focus. She rolled over and moaned. Excruciating pain cut across her chest and her head was pounding. A burning sensation radiated across her right shoulder. Someone was wiping her forehead with a cool damp cloth.

"Caroline, you have to wake up."

Caroline kept her eyes closed, ignoring the voice.

"Caroline, please wake up."

The voice was insistent and kept calling her name over and over. She groaned and slowly opened her eyes. Grandpa, or someone who looked just like him, was sitting in a chair next to her bed. She stared in amazement. His hair was cut short, light brown peppered with white. He was wearing eyeglasses and a freshly ironed shirt and new Levi's.

"You have to stay awake, Caroline, you have a bad concussion."

Caroline looked around the room in fascination. She was in her bedroom, yet nothing was the same. The walls were painted a light fern green and there was a new dark oak desk in the corner, with shelves of books lining the wall. In the corner was a cupboard with rows of trophies on display.

Suddenly, the door swung open and Pete strolled into the room. The first thing Caroline noticed was that he was not limping. He didn't look any different, but he was wearing a bright red shirt, instead of his subdued tones he usually wore, and around his waist was a belt with a huge silver buckle. There was a bucking bull etched in the middle and the words, "First Prize, Bull Riding, 1916, Calgary Stampede."

"Good, you're awake," he said brightly, as he approached the bed and looked down at her.

"Hi," Caroline answered almost shyly. "Where am I?"

Grandpa looked at Pete in consternation. "Maybe we should call Doc Adams." he said anxiously.

"She took a pretty good bump to her head," Pete said consolingly. "I'm sure she'll be right as rain in no time."

"Just to be safe, I'm giving Doc a call."

"He just left here a little while ago. Remember, he told us she might be confused when she first woke up. Maybe we should get her something to eat or drink."

"Do you want anything, Caroline?" Grandpa asked.

"Just some water, please."

"I'll run downstairs and fill the pitcher," Pete offered, as he turned and left the room.

"You sure gave us a scare," Grandpa said to Caroline as he dunked the cloth in the cool water and then laid it across her forehead.

"What happened?"

"Don't you remember anything?"

"I remember riding Ebony down the path and he tripped over a root. Is he okay?" Caroline asked, attempting to sit up. Her head started spinning and a sharp pain made her gasp.

"Now, just you lay back and relax," Grandpa said gently. "And what in the world are you talking about? Ebony's fine."

Caroline lay back on her pillow. "It's my fault. I should have been paying closer attention."

"It could have happened to anyone. You just took the corner too tightly."

"How did you find me?"

"Pete and I were working in the barn, and we heard you crash when you fell. You hit the corral gate pretty hard."

"My head and ribs hurt."

"I wouldn't wonder. You broke two ribs, tore a couple of shoulder muscles and have a huge whopping concussion."

"Grandpa I'm so sorry I ran away."

Grandpa looked at her enquiringly. Pete had just returned to the bedroom and had overheard her comment.

"That's it, Pete, I'm calling Dr. Adams back. Now she's talking nonsense about having run away and something about Ebony tripping on a root."

"Caroline, don't you remember anything that happened before your accident?" Pete asked, setting the pitcher down on the table.

"Not everything, but I remember overhearing you and Grandpa having a big fight and about the fire..."

"I don't recall having any fight, do you, Pete?" Grandpa asked.

"Nope, and I don't recall anything about a fire, either."

Seeing the concerned looks on Grandpa and Pete's faces, Caroline decided it was best to change the topic.

"Whose trophies are those?" she asked, pointing at the shelf.

"Okay, that's it. I'm calling Dr. Adams right away. You keep an eye on her, Pete." With those words, Grandpa left the room and scurried downstairs to the kitchen.

Pete sat down on the edge of Caroline's bed and poured her a glass of water. She sipped it slowly.

"Maybe for a while you shouldn't talk about what happened. I think in time, matters will straighten themselves out and eventually you'll forget certain things and start recalling new things."

Caroline raised her head and looked into Pete's eyes. It was like looking into a deep well. She nodded, handing him back the glass of water.

"And by the way, those trophies are yours. You and Ebony won them in barrel racing."

"We did?"

"That's what you were doing when you had your accident. You were practicing in the corral and got thrown."

"Grandpa didn't sell Ebony to Mr. Mitchell, then?"

"Now, why would your Grandpa sell the best quarter horse in the country to Mitchell?"

"To pay the taxes on the ranch."

Pete laughed and then shook his head in amusement. "Except for Leonard Mitchell's place, Eagle Ridge Ranch is one of the largest and most prosperous ranches in Alberta. Our quarter horses are the best in the country. It's all thanks to Ebony."

Before Caroline could ask any more questions, the sound of Grandpa's footsteps were heard coming up the stairs. Pete raised his finger to his lips and Caroline immediately changed the topic.

"Is Grandpa still the same as he was, you know, angry all the time?"

"When you got hurt, he was pretty worried. He's been like a fussy old mother hen."

Caroline grinned, trying to picture Grandpa in that role. She wondered what other changes she would find when she was finally able to get up and move around. Was this what Sarah had foreseen, what she knew would happen if Caroline succeeded in her undertaking?

Grandpa entered the bedroom and sat down in the chair, a relieved look on his face. "Dr. Adams says you'll be okay, says it's because of the concussion. You have to get some rest now, but we're going to have to wake you up every two hours for the rest of the night."

"Fine, I'll take first watch," Pete said looking over at Grandpa. "You best get some rest. I'll be waking you in a few hours."

"I suppose I should get some shuteye," Grandpa said, as he stood up and walked over to the door. At the last second, he turned and looked at Caroline. "That young boyfriend of yours will be calling in the morning before the rooster wakes up."

"Boyfriend?"

"You can worry about Scott tomorrow," Pete interrupted quickly, before Caroline started asking questions that would have Grandpa running downstairs to call Dr. Adams again.

Chapter 21
A Different Time and a Better Place

It was a long night with Grandpa and Pete continuously waking her up every two hours. Early in the morning, Caroline thankfully fell into an exhausted sleep. She could not forget the fire and Hannah's screams. She kept reliving them over and over in her head.

It was late afternoon by the time she woke. Pete had just walked into her bedroom to check on her and she shyly asked him where her chamber pot was. Grinning from ear to ear, he helped her into her robe then led her into one of the rooms across the hallway. It had been converted into a bathroom and Caroline stared in amazement.

Walking over to the sink, she turned on the water, her eyes sparkling. "When did we get indoor plumbing?" She asked.

"About five years ago. I imagine a lot of things will have changed. When you're up and walking, I'll give you a tour."

On her way back to her bedroom Caroline noticed the storage room next to Grandpa's bedroom had a bed, cupboards, and a shelf lined with trophies. She looked enquiringly at Pete asking him whose room it was.

"Mine."

"Don't you sleep in the bunkhouse anymore?" Caroline asked, noticing the amused look on his face.

"Don't believe I ever did. That's for the hired hands, not family."

"Are those your trophies?"

"Yup, two for bronco riding and the big one for bull riding."

"Is that where you got that silver buckle?"

"You bet. First place at the Calgary Stampede."

"Your limp is gone, so you weren't injured?"

"Reckon my life changed considerably and for the better," Pete said as he led Caroline back to her room.

It was another two days before Caroline was able to get out of bed and move around on her own without assistance.

The first thing she did was take out her jewellery box and look inside. She found her locket and lying next to it was the silver broach.

Grandpa strolled into the room and walked over and looked over her shoulder. "Hmm, you still got that old locket of your Grandma's?"

"You know how important it is to me?"

"I reckon I do, but not as important as your horse broach?"

"Why would you say that?"

"I suppose when Scott gave it to you he knew how much you would cherish it seeing as how it belonged to your mom. Your mom and dad and his parents were the best of friends, they were inseparable. When your mom died your dad gave the broach to Sharon. I remember he asked me if I should keep it for you, but I told him to do what he felt was right."

Caroline felt as if the floor was opening up under her. She gripped the broach tightly in her hands. " Funny how things come around full circle isn't it?"

Grandpa grunted, and Caroline smiled. She was glad he hadn't changed completely. Being grumpy was entirely different than being mean.

After Grandpa left the room, Caroline went and looked out her window. The lawn was lush and green, flowers growing everywhere. A thick hedge of lilacs lined the roadway. The barn had a new roof and was painted a bright red. The bunkhouse was in the same place as the old one had been, but this one was freshly painted and had large windows and a porch. There were horses in the pasture and she noticed cowhands coming in and out of the barn.

There was a second bathroom on the main floor, but the kitchen was the most surprising of all. The old wood stove, which Caroline knew without a doubt was Annie's, had been cleaned, repainted, and had been converted over to electricity. There was a kitchen sink with running water and a refrigerator where the old ice box had been. She wandered over to the door leading down to the root cellar and turned on the light. She walked carefully down the steps and then stopped when she got to the bottom. The shelves were stocked with canned and preserved food, and the bins were half full of vegetables from the garden. She walked over to the far corner, but the old trunk was gone.

Her next stop was the living room. Over the fireplace was a wedding picture of her parents. Her mother was wearing a beautiful white gown with a long white veil. Her hands, folded in front of her, held a bouquet of lilacs. Sitting on the fireplace mantel was the sunflower canister and next to it was Hannah's journal. In the corner next to the book shelves was a TV set, something she had thought they would never own.

Caroline wandered over to the piano. There were a number of framed pictures sitting on top. She recognized the family portrait of Annie, Grandpa and the rest of his family, but she found it difficult to look at. It was too soon.

Pete entered the room and came and stood behind her. Grandpa was setting up a lounge chair for Caroline on the porch. She had told him she was feeling much better and had pleaded with him to stop fussing, but he had insisted she relax and not walk around too much.

"Everything is different, ain't it?" he asked quietly.

"But so much better, Pete," Caroline said, grateful she was able to talk to someone about it.

"I notice you watching your Grandpa a lot, has he really changed that much?"

Caroline slowly nodded her head. "Can I ask you

something about my parents?"

"Sure."

"Did my Dad and Grandpa ever make up?"

"Don't recollect that they ever had a fight. Your pa left home after he graduated and moved to Red Deer. He never did take to ranching, so he found a job in some fancy bank. Met your mother there and although they didn't have much time together, they were happy."

"I'm glad to hear that, Pete."

"They came and visited a lot and always made a point of seeing the Chalmers'. Your Pa loved the land as much as your grandparents did, just didn't want to ranch it."

"I wish I could have known them."

"Your mother's death was hard on everyone. I never saw a couple dote so much time on a child as your Grandpa and Grandma did when you came to live with them. The telegram saying that your Pa had died arrived a few days afore the War ended."

For the longest time, Pete said nothing. "Caroline, I can't begin to think of what things were like before and I can't rightly say I understand exactly what happened."

"You saw me that day, at the fire, didn't you?"

"At first, I thought you were Sarah and that she had come back to give us a message. Spent most of my growing up years believing that was the case."

"How long did it take for you to realize it was me?"

"Not until you started to get older and I realized how much you looked like her. I finally put everything together when you started wearing Levi's and cowboy boots. Don't recollect Sarah ever wearing anything like that."

Caroline smiled at her old friend. "I'm just glad you realized how important it was that someone had to look inside the canister."

"At first, I wasn't sure I was seeing right. You were

disappearing right before my eyes. Thought I was going crazy, but when the canister didn't fade, I figured it was the reason you were there. It had to be important."

"I was so worried that you wouldn't figure it out."

"I took the canister to Eric and told him to look inside. I guess he must have seen how serious I was, because he did just that."

"So, he read the journal and realized that the fire was a terrible, unfortunate tragedy."

"Took your Grandpa a while to accept what happened, but he finally come to terms with it all."

"Pete, when I heard you and Grandpa talking about the fire, when I galloped out of the yard, I saw you standing on the porch watching me go. Why didn't you try to stop me?"

"I knew you had to do this on your own and that I must not interfere. It was because of your courage and your love for your Grandpa that you succeeded."

"Thank you so much for all you have done," Caroline said, as she leaned over and kissed Pete on his cheek.

"Like I said, I can't begin to understand what you've been through and I won't ask, unless you want to talk about it, then I'll be here for you."

"Thanks, Pete, but I do have one very important question."

"What might that be?"

"Do you still play Lonesome Checkers?"

"Yup, and I always win."

Caroline chuckled quietly. Together she and Pete walked out to the porch to join Grandpa, ready to face the future together.

Epilogue

The sun broke through the clouds and Caroline inhaled deeply, savouring the pungent scent of the pines.

"Hey, wait up for me," a voice called from behind. Caroline stopped Ebony and waited until Scott caught up with them. He reached over and tugged her hat down over her eyes. Caroline grinned and took his hand.

"Are you getting tired?" Scott asked. This is the first time you've done any hard riding since your accident?"

"Scott, I'm fine. If I had spent another day in that house being smothered by Grandpa and Pete, I'd have gone crazy."

"Where did they go?"

"They're just a little ways ahead. I think Grandpa wanted to have a look around before we all arrived."

"I can't believe he's never returned to his old homestead since he was fifteen years old. What made him decide to do it now?"

The path narrowed and Caroline released Scott's hand. He eased Monty in behind Ebony and they continued riding in single file. Caroline looked down and smiled at the necklace hanging around her neck. It was a tiny golden chain that held a small ring. Scott had asked her to go steady last week and Grandpa had agreed as long as they waited until she turned sixteen before they went on a date alone. Both Caroline and Scott had readily agreed.

"He asked me what I wanted for my birthday and I told him I wanted to see where he was born," Caroline said, twisting in the saddle so that she faced Scott. "I told you about what had happened when he was fifteen, about his sister and grandmother dying in the fire."

Scott nodded and for a while they rode in silence. Eventually, they arrived at the fork and Ebony automatically turned right.

"You'd almost think he knew where he was going," Scott commented.

"I always told you he was smarter than that old plug of yours," Caroline replied jokingly.

Scott grunted in reply.

Caroline's stomach was tied up in knots. Sometimes the memories were sharp and vivid, while at times they were fleeting images, almost as if they had never happened.

When they arrived at the mountain ash, she left the path and rode towards the clearing. She gently kneed Ebony, wondering how he would react.

Ebony did not hesitate. He trotted boldly into the open, with Monty following closely behind. Grandpa and Pete were standing in the spot where the house had stood.

The two men turned when they heard them approach. Pete saw the look on Caroline's face and he gestured for Scott to follow him over to the creek. Scott dismounted Monty and they wandered over to the far side of the meadow, talking quietly.

"This is where the house used to be," Grandpa said, poking the toe of his boot into the soil. "And over there was the chicken coop. Behind it was the barn."

Caroline dismounted and joined Grandpa where he was standing next to the charred remains of the fireplace. The only indication a house had once stood in this spot were a few blackened boards buried in the tall grass. For the briefest second, Caroline expected to look up and see Annie and Hannah sitting on the porch.

Suddenly she gasped, bent over and slowly stood up. She showed Grandpa the sprig of blossoms she was clasping tightly in her hands.

"Now, if that don't beat all," he said shaking his head in amazement. "Imagine lilacs growing this late in the year."

Caroline followed Grandpa around the field, stopping when he did and listening when something triggered his memory. He talked about his horse Buck and his little sister Hannah. He told her about Pete, when he had come into their lives, and how they had become as close as brothers.

Eventually, they arrived at the hill where the root cellar had been located. The door had rotted and fallen off its hinges. Caroline poked her head inside but the dirt walls had collapsed long ago. Most of the dugout was buried under mud and rocks.

"That's the root cellar," Grandpa said. "Hannah used to hide in there when Granny was looking for her to do chores. Course, she always found her."

Caroline swallowed, willing herself to laugh at Grandpa's story.

"We better start back," Grandpa said. "Wesley and Suzanne will be picking you two up in a few hours and if you plan on driving to Olds to catch a movie, you don't want to be late."

"Grandpa, thanks for bringing me here. I know how hard this must be for you and for Pete."

"I always meant to come back, but before you know it, you're an old man wondering where the time went."

"I love this meadow. It's so beautiful and peaceful."

"I've been thinking about it a lot lately. For some reason, I can't seem to get it out of my head," Grandpa said as he turned and strolled over to the horses where Pete and Scott were waiting.

"I know exactly what you mean," Caroline whispered under her breath.

Everyone mounted and the two older men rode ahead while Caroline took up the rear behind Scott. She had wrapped the lilacs in her bandanna and had gently laid them in her saddlebag.

Lowering her hand, she reached inside her pocket.

She touched a pair of gold rimmed bifocals. The lens was cracked and the frame was crusted with dirt. She had found them lying next to the lilacs, but had said nothing to Grandpa, understanding this was a precious gift for her alone.

For a brief second, she thought she heard the soft strumming of a guitar and the sound of a child's laughter. Smiling, she let the branches fall gently behind her as she rode to catch up with the others.

THE END

About the author

Shirley Bigelow DeKelver was born in Calgary, Alberta. After working over forty years as a paralegal, she and her husband Don retired to White Lake, a fishing lake located in the Interior of British Columbia. *Lilacs and Bifocals* is Shirley's second published young adult novel, her first being an adventure story entitled *The Trouble with Mandy*. She is an avid photographer and enjoys acrylic painting. You can visit her website at www.shirleydekelver.com.

If you enjoyed this book, you might also like:

Always & Forever
By: Diana Harrison

Jon Burton thinks he's having a nightmare but the bad dreams don't fade when he's awake.

Callie, his girlfriend, mother of his son Oliver, has been killed in a road accident.

Now he faces life as a single parent.

He's at school taking his A levels.

He wants to go to Uni.

His mother has her own life and career.

His sister, Fay, older and wiser perhaps' advises him to have the baby adopted. Get on with his life.

He should do that.

Callie doesn’t want him to do that. Only her body is dead. Her spirit is still alive. And she wants Jon, Oliver, and her to stay together.

Always & Forever.

An Element of Time
By: Bebe Knight

A vampire and a slayer walk into a bar… Sounds like the beginning of a bad joke, but for Veronica and Mackenzie, it’s the beginning of the rest of their lives…

The world has seen its fair share of evil, but Veronica Chase had no idea such monsters truly existed. Werewolves, poltergeists, witches… even vampires. Ignorance was bliss. But her reality was crushed on that horrid day her family was taken away from her. Now, Veronica has devoted her entire life to hunting those very creatures, searching for the werewolf pack that murdered her parents in hopes of finding her abducted sister. Nothing will get in her way of settling the score for the hand she was unjustly dealt. That is until her newest assignment brings her to her knees.

After one hundred and eight years on earth, Mackenzie Jones thought he had seen it all. With the exception of daylight of course, but that's what comes with the territory being a vampire and all. Perpetually damned to live his life as a bartender in the shadows of the night, nothing has sparked his interest lately. Just once he wished something exciting would happen in his mundane life. Little did he know, his wish was about to come true. Walking through the door to his bar, and into his heart, Mackenzie allows love to take the wheel for the first time. There's just one slight problem. She's there to kill him.

Made in the USA
San Bernardino, CA
05 May 2016